£2.49

Hushabye

A Kate Redman Mystery: Book 1

Celina Grace

Hushabye
(A Kate Redman Mystery: Book 1)

A MISSING BABY. A MURDERED girl. A case where everyone has something to hide...

On the first day of her new job in the West Country, Detective Sergeant Kate Redman finds herself investigating the kidnapping of Charlie Fullman, the newborn son of a wealthy entrepreneur and his trophy wife. It seems a straightforward case... but as Kate and her fellow officer Mark Olbeck delve deeper, they uncover murky secrets and multiple motives for the crime.

Kate finds the case bringing up painful memories of her own past secrets. As she confronts the truth about herself, her increasing emotional instability threatens both her hard-won career success and the possibility that they will ever find Charlie Fullman alive...

Hushabye is the first in the **Kate Redman Mysteries** series from crime writer Celina Grace, author of **Lost Girls** and **The House on Fever Street**.

Prologue

CASEY FULLMAN OPENED HER EYES and knew something was wrong.

It was too bright. She was used to waking to grey dimness, the before-sunrise hours of a winter morning. Dita would stand by the bed with Charlie in one arm, a warmed bottle in the other. Casey would struggle up to a sitting position, trying to avoid the jab of pain from her healing Caesarean scar, and take the baby and the bottle.

You're mad to get up so early when you don't have to, her mother had told her, more than once. *It's not like you're breastfeeding. Let Dita do it.* But Casey, smiling and shrugging, would never give up those first waking moments. She enjoyed the delicious warmth of the baby snuggled against her body, his dark eyes fixed upon hers as he sucked furiously at the bottle.

She didn't envy Dita, though, stumbling back to bed through the early morning dark to her bedroom next to the nursery. Casey would have gotten up herself to take Charlie from his cot when he cried for his food, but Nick needed his sleep, and it seemed to work out better all round for Dita, so close to the cot anyway, to bring him and the bottle into the bedroom instead. *That's what I pay her for*, Nick had said, when she'd suggested getting up herself.

But this morning there was no Dita, sleepy-eyed in rumpled pyjamas, standing by the bed. There was no Charlie. Casey sat up sharply, wincing as her stomach muscles pulled at the scar. She looked over at Nick, fast asleep next to her. Sleeping like a baby. But where was her baby, her Charlie?

She got up and padded across the soft, expensive, sound-muffling carpet, not bothering with her dressing gown, too anxious now to delay. It was almost full daylight; she could see clearly. The bedroom door was shut, and she opened it to a silent corridor outside.

The door to Dita's room was standing open, but the door to Charlie's nursery was closed. Casey looked in Dita's room. Her nanny's bed was empty, the room in its usual mess, clothes and toys all over the floor. She must have gone into Charlie's room. They must both be in there. Why hadn't Dita brought him through? *He must be ill*, thought Casey, and fear broke over her like a wave. Her palm slipped on the door handle to the nursery.

She pushed the door. It stuck, halfway open. Casey shoved harder and it moved, opening wide enough for her to see an out-flung arm on the carpet, a hand half-curled. Her throat closed up. Frantically, she pushed at the door, and it opened far enough to enable her to squeeze inside.

It was Dita she saw first, spread-eagled on the floor, face upwards. For a split second, Casey thought, crazily, that it was a model of her nanny, a waxwork, something that someone had left in the room for a joke. Dita's face was pale as colourless candle wax, but that wasn't the worst thing. There was something wrong with the structure of her face, her forehead dented, her nose pushed to one side. Her thick blonde hair was fanned out around her head like the stringy petals of a giant flower.

Casey felt her heartbeat falter as she looked down at the body. She was dimly aware that her lungs felt as if they'd seized up, frozen solid. She mouthed like a fish, gasping for air, but it wasn't until she moved her gaze from Dita to look at Charlie's cot that she began to scream.

Chapter One

KATE REDMAN STOOD IN THE tiny hallway of her flat and regarded herself in the full-length mirror that hung beside the front door. She never left the flat without giving herself a quick once-over—not for reasons of vanity, but to check that all was in place.She smoothed down her hair and tugged at her jacket, pulling the shoulders more firmly into shape. Her bag stood by the front door mat. She picked it up and checked her purse and mobile and warrant card were all there, zipped away in the inner pocket.

She was early, but then she was always early. Time for a quick coffee before the doorbell was expected to ring? She walked into the small, neat kitchen, her hand hovering over the kettle. She decided against it. She felt jittery enough already. *Calm down, Kate.*

It was awful being the new girl; it was like being back at school again. Although now at least, she was well-dressed, with clean hair and clean shoes.

It was fairly unlikely that any of her new co-workers would tell her that she smelt and had nits.

Kate shook herself mentally. She was talking to herself again, the usual internal monologue, always a sign of stress. *It's just a new job. You can do it. They picked you, remember?*

She checked her watch. He was late, although not by much. The traffic at this time of day was always awful. She walked from the kitchen to the lounge – *living room, Kate, living room* – a matter of ten steps. She closed her bedroom door, and then opened it again to let the air flow in. She walked back to the hallway just as the doorbell finally rang. She took a deep breath and fixed her smile in place before she opened it.

"DS Redman?" asked the man on the doorstep. "I'm DS Olbeck. Otherwise known as Mark. Bloody awful parking around here. Sorry I'm late."

Kate noted a few things immediately: the fact that he'd said 'bloody,' whereas every other copper she'd ever known would have said 'fucking'; his slightly too long dark hair; that he had a nice, crinkle-eyed smile. She felt a bit better.

"No drama," she said breezily. "I'm ready. Call me Kate."

When they got to the car, she hesitated slightly for a moment, unsure of whether she should clear the passenger seat of all the assorted crap that was piled upon it or whether she should leave it to Mark.

He muttered an apology and threw everything into the back.

"I'm actually quite neat," he said, swinging the door open for her, "but it doesn't seem to extend to the car, if you see what I mean."

Kate smiled politely. As he swung the car out into the road, she fixed her mind on the job ahead of them.

"Can you tell me–" she began, just as he began to ask her a question.

"You're from–"

"Oh, sorry–"

"I was going to say, you're up from Bournemouth, aren't you?" Olbeck asked.

"That's right. I grew up there."

"I thought that's where people went to retire."

Kate grinned. "Pretty much. There's wasn't a lot of, shall we say, *life* when I was growing up." She paused. "Still, we had the beach. Where are you from?"

"London," said DS Olbeck, briefly. There was a pause while he waited to join the dual carriageway. "Nowhere glamorous. Just the outskirts, really. Ruislip, Middlesex. How are you finding the move to the West Country?"

"Fine so far."

"Have you got family around here?

Kate was growing impatient with the small talk.

"No, no one around here," she said. "Can I ask you about the case?"

"Of course."

"I know it's a murder and kidnap case–"

"Yes. The child – baby – belongs to the Fullmans. Nick Fullman is a very wealthy entrepreneur, made most of his cash in property development. He got married about a year ago – to one of those sort of famous people."

"How do you mean?" Kate asked.

"Oh you know, the sort of Z-list celebrity that keeps showing up in Heat magazine. Her name's Casey Bright. Well, Casey Fullman now. Appeared in Okay when they got married, showing you round their lovely home, you know the sort of thing."

Kate smiled. "I get the picture."

She wouldn't have pegged DS Olbeck for a gossip mag reader, but then people often weren't what they seemed.

"And the murder?"

"The nanny, Dita Olgweisch. Looks incidental to the kidnapping at this point, but you never know. What *is* known is that the baby is missing and as it – he's – only three months old, you can imagine the kind of thing we're dealing with here."

"Yes." Kate was silent for a moment. A three-month-old baby...memories threatened to surface and she pushed them away. "So on the face of it, we're looking at the baby was snatched, the nanny interrupted whoever it was, and she was killed?"

"Like you say, on the surface, that seems to be what's happened. We'll know more soon. We'll be there in," he glanced at the sat nav on the windscreen, "fifteen minutes or so."

They were off the motorway now and into the countryside. Looking out of the window, Kate noted the ploughed fields, shorn of the autumn stubble, the skeletal shapes of the trees. It was a grey January day, the sky like a flat blanket the colour of nothing. *The worst time of year*, she thought, *everything dead, shut down for the winter, months until spring.*

The car slowed, turned into a driveway, and continued through formidable iron gates which were opened for them by a uniformed officer. After they drove through, Kate looked back to see the gates swung shut behind them. She noted the high wooden fence that ran alongside the road, the CCTV camera on the gatepost. The driveway wound though dripping trees and opened out into a courtyard at the front of the house.

"Looks like security is a priority," she said to her companion as he pulled the car up by the front door.

He raised his eyebrows. "Clearly not enough of a priority."

"Well, we'll see," said Kate.

They both got out of the car. There was another uniformed officer by the front door, a pale redhead whose nose had reddened in the raw air. He was stamping his feet and swinging his arms but stopped abruptly when Kate and Olbeck reached him.

"DCI Anderton here yet?" said Olbeck.

"Yes sir. He's inside, in the kitchen. Just go straight through the hallway."

They stepped inside. The hallway was cavernous, tiled in chilly white stone, scuffed and marked now with the imprint of shoes and boots. Kate looked around. A staircase split in two and flowed around the upper reaches of the hallway to the first floor of the house. There was an enormous light shade suspended from the ceiling, a tangled mass of glass tubing and metal filaments. It had probably cost more than her flat, but she thought it hideous all the same. The house was warm, too warm; the underfloor heating was obviously at full blast, but there was an atmosphere of frigidity nonetheless. Perhaps it was the glossy white floor, the high ceilings, the general air of too much space. A Philip Starke chair stood against the wall, looking as though it had been carved out of ice.

"Mark? That you? Through here."

They followed the shout through into the kitchen, big on an industrial scale. It opened out into a glass-walled conservatory, which overlooked a terrace leading down to a clipped and manicured lawn. Detective Chief Inspector Anderton stood by a cluster of leather sofas where a woman was sitting, crouching forward, her long blonde hair dipping towards the floor. Kate looked around her surreptitiously. The place stank of money, *new* money: wealth just about dripped from the ceilings. It *must* be a kidnapping. *Now, Kate*, she chided herself. *No jumping to conclusions*.

She had only met the Chief Inspector once before, at her interview. He was a grey man: steel grey hair, dark grey eyes, grey suit. Easy to dismiss, at first.

"Ah, DS Redman," he said as they both approached. "Welcome. Hoping to catch up with you later in my office, but we'll have to see how things go. You can see how things are here."

He gave her a firm handshake, holding her gaze for a moment. She was surprised at the sudden tug of her lower belly, a pulse that vanished almost as soon as she'd registered it. A little shaken, it took her a moment to collect herself. The other two officers had begun talking to the blonde woman on the sofa. Kate joined them.

Casey Fullman was a tiny woman, very childlike in spite of the bleached hair, the breast implants and the false nails. Kate noted the delicate bones of her wrist and ankles. Casey had bunchy cheeks, smooth and round like the curve of a peach, a tip-tilted nose and large blue eyes. These last were bloodshot, tears glistening along the edge of her reddened eyelids.

"I don't know," she was saying as Kate joined them. Her voice was high, and she spoke with a gasp that could have been tears but might be habitual. "I don't know. I didn't hear anything and when I woke up, Dita," she drew in her breath, "Dita wasn't there. She would normally be there with a bottle and Ch- and Ch-"

She broke down entirely, dropping her head down to her bare knees. There was a moment of silence while Kate watched the ends of Casey's long hair touch the floor.

Anderton began to utter some soothing words. Kate looked around, her eye attracted by a movement outside on the terrace. A man was walking up and down, talking into a mobile phone, his free hand gesticulating wildly. As Kate watched, he flipped the phone closed and turned towards the house. He was young, good-looking and, somewhat incongruously given the early hour, dressed in a suit.

"Sorry about that, I had to take it," said Nick Fullman as he entered the room. Kate mentally raised her eyebrows, wondering at a man who prioritised a phone call, presumably a business matter, over comforting his wife after their baby son had been kidnapped. *Not necessarily a kidnapping, Kate, stop jumping to conclusions*. She thought she saw an answering disapproval in Olbeck's face.

Anderton introduced his colleagues. Nick Fullman shook hands with them both, rather to

Kate's surprise, and then finally sat down next to his sobbing wife.

"Come on, Case," he said, pulling her up and encircling her with one arm. "Try and keep it together. The police are here to help."

Casey put shaking fingers up to her mouth. She appeared to be trying to control her tears, taking in deep, shuddering breaths.

"Perhaps you'd like a cup of tea?" said Olbeck. He caught Kate's eye, and she immediately looked away. *Don't you bloody dare ask me to make it.* He looked around rather helplessly. "Is there anyone who could , er–"

"I'll make it."

They all looked around at the sound of the words. A woman had come into the kitchen. Or had she? Kate wondered whether she'd been there all along, unnoticed. There was something unmemorable about her, which was odd because she too was dressed in full business attire, her face heavily made-up, her hair straightened and twisted and pinned in an elaborate style on the top of her head.

"This is my PA, Gemma Phillips," said Fullman. There was just a shade of relief in his voice. "Gemma, thanks for coming so quickly."

"It's fine," she said with a brilliant smile, a smile that faded a little as she surveyed Casey, huddled and gasping. "It's terrible. I came as quickly as I could. I can't believe it."

"If you could make tea for us all, that would be wonderful, Miss Phillips," said Anderton.

"It's *Ms* Phillips, if you don't mind," she said, rather quickly. "Or you can call me Gemma. I don't mind."

Anderton inclined his head.

"Of course. We'd like to talk to you as well, once we've been able to sit with Mr and Mrs Fullman for a while."

He turned back to the Fullmans. Gemma shrugged and began to make tea, moving quickly about the room. Kate watched her. Clearly Gemma knew her way around the kitchen very well. What, exactly, was her relationship with her employers like? Had she worked for them long? Presumably she didn't live on the premises. Kate made mental notes to use in her interview with the girl later.

The tea was made and presented to them all. Casey took one sip of hers and choked.

"Oh, sorry," said Gemma. "I always forget you don't take sugar."

There was something in her voice that made Kate's internal sensor light up. Not mockery, not exactly. There was *something* though. Kate scribbled more mental notes.

Nick Fullman had been given coffee, rather than tea, in an elegant white china cup. He'd swallowed it in three gulps. Kate noted the dark shadows under his eyes and the faint jittery shudder of his fingers. A caffeine addict? An insomniac? Or something else?

"I heard nothing," he was saying in response to Anderton's question. "I was sleeping. I sleep pretty heavily, and the first I knew about anything was Casey screaming down the hallway. I ran down and saw, well, saw Dita on the floor. "

"Do you have any theories as to who might have taken your son?"

Casey let out a small moan. Nick pulled her closer to him.

"None whatsoever. I can't believe anyone–" His voice faltered for a second. "I can't believe anyone would do such a thing."

"No one has made any threats against you or your family recently?"

"Of course not."

"Who has access to the house? Do you keep any staff?"

Fullman frowned. "What do you mean by access?"

"Well, keys specifically. But also anyone who is permitted to enter the house, particularly on a regular basis."

"I'll have to think." Fullman was silent for a moment. He looked at his personal assistant.

"Gemma, you couldn't be a star and make another coffee, could you?"

"Of course." Gemma almost jumped from her chair to fulfil his request.

Fullman turned back to the police officers.

"Casey and I have keys, of course. Gemma has a set to the house, although not to the outbuildings, I don't think."

"That's right," called Gemma from the kitchen. "Just the house."

"What about Miss Olgweisch?"

Fullman dropped his eyes to the floor. "Yes, Dita had a full set."

"Anyone else?"

Casey raised her head from her husband's shoulder.

"My mum's got a front door key," she said, her voice hoarse. "She knows the key codes and all that."

"Ah, yes," said Anderton. "The security. Presumably all the people who have keys also have security codes and so forth?"

Fullman nodded. "That's right. There's an access code on the main gate and the alarm code for the house."

Kate and Olbeck exchanged glances. Whoever had taken the baby hadn't set off any of the alarms.

Casey pushed herself upright.

"What are you doing to find him?" she begged.

CELINA GRACE

"Why are we sat here answering all these questions when we should be out there looking for him?"

"Mrs Fullman," said Anderton in a steady tone. "I really do know how desperate you must be feeling. My officers are out there on your land combing every inch of it for clues to Charlie's whereabouts. We just have to try and ascertain a few basic facts so we can think of the best way to move forward as quickly as possible."

"It's just..." Casey's voice trailed away. Kate addressed her husband.

"Mr Fullman, is there anyone who could come and give your wife some support? Give you both some support? Her mother, perhaps?"

Fullman grimaced. "I suppose so. Case, shall I ring your mum?" His wife nodded, mutely, and he stood up. "I'll go and ring her then."

He headed back outside to the terrace, clearly relieved to be escaping the kitchen. Olbeck looked at Kate and raised his eyebrows very slightly. She nodded, just as subtly.

"You two look around," said Anderton. "DS Redman, I'd like you to talk to Ms Phillips once you're done. DS Olbeck, go and see how the search is progressing. I want the neighbours questioned before too long."

The house was newly built, probably less than ten years old. It was a sprawling low building, cedar-clad and white-rendered, technically built on several different levels but as the ground had been dug away and landscaped around it, the house looked like nothing so much as a very expensive bungalow. Or so Kate thought, walking around the perimeter with Olbeck. They had checked the layout of the bedrooms, noting the distance of the baby's nursery from the Fullman's bedroom.

"Why wasn't the baby in their room?" asked Kate.

Olbeck glanced at her. "Should he have been?"

"I think that's the standard advice. Everyone I know with tiny babies keeps them in their own bedrooms. Sometimes in their beds. Not stuck down the end of the corridor."

"I don't know," said Olbeck. "The nanny was right next door."

Dita Olgweisch's room and the nursery were still sealed off by the Scene of Crime team gathering evidence. Kate stood back for a second to let a SOCO past her, rustling along in white overalls.

"I'll ask Mrs Fullman when she's feeling up to it," she said. "Perhaps there was a simple explanation."

The view from the terrace was undeniably lovely. The ground dropped steeply away from the decking and the lawn ended in a semi-circle of woodland; beech, ash, and oak trees all stood as if on guard around the grass. Kate could see the movements of the uniformed officers as they carried out their fingertip search. Olbeck came up beside her and they both stood looking out on the scene. Kate wondered if he was thinking what she was thinking – that somewhere out in those peaceful looking woods was a tiny child's body. Her stomach clenched.

"I've never worked on a child case before," said Olbeck abruptly. Kate turned her head, surprised. "Murder, obviously. But never a child."

"We don't know that the baby's..." Kate didn't want to finish the sentence.

"I know." They were both silent for a moment. "I hope you're right. God, I hope you're right."

There didn't seem to be much else to say. They both had things to do, but for another moment, they stood quietly, side by side, looking out at the swaying, leafless branches of the trees.

Chapter Two

KATE FOUND GEMMA PHILLIPS IN what was clearly a home office, one of the smaller rooms off a corridor leading from the kitchen. There were two desks, filing cabinets, a printer and several swivel chairs. Gemma was typing busily on the keyboard of a laptop. As Kate got closer, though, she could see that all the girl was doing was updating her Facebook status. *What was she putting in her update*? Kate wondered. *Gemma Phillips...is about to be interviewed by the police.*

"Hi Gemma," she said, grabbing one of the swivel chairs and turning it to face Gemma's desk. "I'd like to have a chat, ask you a few questions, if I may?"

"No problem," said Gemma, but rather uneasily. Her long fingernails clicked on the edge of her laptop.

"You've worked for Mr Fullman for how long?"

"Um, seven years. Almost eight years."

"Quite a while then. What's he like to work for? Is he a good boss?"

Gemma looked even more uneasy. "He's okay. Bit of a slave driver, sometimes, but they all are, aren't they?"

Kate repressed her answer, which was something along the lines of no, she wouldn't know, having never been a secretary, thank God. That was mean and snobbish of her. What in God's name did she have to be snobbish about?

"Could you tell me more about him? I know he's in property development. What sort of thing does he do?"

"How do you mean?"

"Well, what sort of thing is he working on at the moment? Any particular project?"

Gemma frowned.

"Well, he's got a big residential building contract on the go. Newbuild flats over in Wallingham. Do you mean that sort of thing?"

"Yes, well–" Kate tried a different tack. "What sort of work do you do for him?"

Gemma looked at her laptop screen.

"I do all sorts. Deal with his diary, deal with his phone calls, arrange his travel. Type up the contracts and deal with the rental agencies."

"Do you do any work for Mrs Fullman?"

"A bit." Gemma sounded resentful. "Since she had the baby, she's been asking me to do more and more. That's always the way. You start off by doing someone a favour and then they take advantage."

She'd referred to the child as the baby, not Charlie. Was that significant?

"Have Mr and Mrs Fullman been married long?" Kate knew they hadn't, but she wanted to try and draw a bit more from Gemma on her employer's wife.

"Not really. Not even a year. She got pregnant before they got married."

"She was a TV star, wasn't she, before she got married?"

Gemma's lip curled. "Well, not really. She was in that reality show about the Mayfair hairdressers, that's all. She did a bit of modelling after that. She wasn't really *famous*. Not an A-lister, or anything." Kate looked her in the eye, and she flushed and dropped her head, obviously aware of the rising tone of her voice. "Anyway, she hasn't done much since the baby came."

"Charlie," said Kate. *He has a name.*

"Yes, Charlie."

Kate paused.

"How did you get on with Dita Olgweisch?"

Gemma looked stricken. Kate saw her throat ripple as she swallowed.

"I can't believe she's dead," she said, almost in a whisper. "I can't - it doesn't seem possible."

"You were close?"

"No, not really. Well, we were friendly. I mean, we'd chat and all that. I didn't really see that much of her. She was always out with the baby –with Charlie." The girl's hands were shaking. "I can't believe she's dead," she repeated.

Her distress seemed genuine. Kate observed her more closely, noting with a stab of pity that despite the carefully applied makeup, the ironed clothes, and the elaborate hairstyle, Gemma was undeniably plain. *Plain*. What a stupid, cruel word – but apt in this instance. There was something forgettable about the girl, something negligible. Was that the root of her resentment against Casey Fullman – the jealousy of the less attractive woman over the prettier one?

"Are you married, Gemma?" she asked suddenly.

Gemma flushed again. "No, I'm not. Why?"

Kate smiled, trying to put her at her ease. "Just being nosy. I'm permanently single myself."

Gemma half-smiled.

"I've got a fella," she said. "We're engaged. Practically engaged."

"Congratulations." Kate paused for a moment. "Anyway, let's talk a bit more about Dita, if it doesn't distress you too much. Are you happy to carry on?" She took the girl's shrug as assent. "How long had she been Charlie's nanny?"

Gemma thought for a moment. "Not long. Only a couple of months."

"Did Mrs Fullman need a lot of help with the baby? He's very young." In her mind's eye, Kate could see a small, crumpled face, eyes tight shut, black birth hair in a fluffy corona. She cleared her throat. "Did – did she have a difficult birth?"

"I don't know," said Gemma, looking offended. "She didn't talk about it with *me*. I don't think she even wanted a nanny, to be honest, Nick is the one who got Dita to come. It's what you do when you're rich, isn't it? Get help even if you don't need it." She clicked her fingernails on the edge of her laptop, an irritating, scuttering sound. "Nick's got money to burn. He just spends it for the sake of it."

Kate nodded. She eased forward and stood up, feeling that she'd got enough to be going on with for a while. Then she sat down again.

"What do you think happened last night, Gemma?" she asked.

"Me?" said Gemma. She looked startled, then frightened. "I don't know. How would I know?"

"Do you have any ideas at all?"

The mascara-laded eyelashes blinked rapidly. Then Gemma turned back to her laptop. Her shoulders were rigid. "Some paedo, wasn't it?" she said. She didn't look at Kate. "You hear about it all the time, paedophiles snatching kids."

"Very rarely babies, and very rarely are children taken from their own beds."

Gemma shrugged, still turned away.

"Well, you asked me what I thought," she said, with some hostility.

Kate stood up again. "And Dita?" she said.

Gemma shot her a hunted glance. Again, she looked frightened.

"I don't know," she said in a small voice. "She must have just got in – in his way."

Chapter Three

KATE AND OLBECK DROVE BACK to the station
in Olbeck's car while Anderton followed them in
his own vehicle. Kate stared unseeing out of the
window at the bleak landscape, her mind running
over her conversation with Gemma.

There was clearly no love lost between Gemma
and her employer's wife, but was that significant?
Probably not. So Casey hadn't wanted a nanny?
Why had Nick employed one? Was it just, as Gemma
suggested, that he could afford it? She dismissed
the thoughts from her mind as they joined the ring
road that encircled the town, knowing that they
were nearly at the station.

Kate looked with interest at the buildings and
people of Abbeyford. She'd taken a risk, taking a job
here – she knew no one, she knew nothing about
the town. Her flat was a good hour and a half's
drive from the police station. Would that become
a problem? She didn't want to leave her flat, she

loved it, but if it was necessary for her career, then that was a step she was willing to take.

Abbeyford was a market town that had grown up around a tiny collection of medieval buildings, the last remnants of a vanished monastery that had once provided alms and charity to the poor of the county. Now the high street was lined with the usual coffee shops, charity shops, supermarkets and the odd, struggling independent store. There was a handsome Victorian town hall, a modern library, two secondary schools, and plenty of good and not-so-good pubs.

At the police station, a charmless, redbrick sixties building, Anderton assembled his team for a debriefing session. Kate, again feeling like the new girl at school, took a seat and fixed her eyes on the DCI. She was bothered again by that flash of attraction she'd had before, when he'd shaken her hand in the Fullmans' kitchen. She made an effort to concentrate on what he was saying.

"We're assuming the murder took place as incidental to the kidnapping," he said, gesturing to the crime scene photographs affixed to the whiteboard. "But should we assume that? Is it possible that the real motive for the crime was the murder of Dita Olgweisch and the kidnapping of Charlie Fullman is incidental to *that*?

"It's possible," said Olbeck. "But where's the motive?"

"Exactly, Mark," said Anderton. "But I'm trying to make it clear that we can't take anything for granted here. It could be a kidnapping for money, although as yet there's been no ransom note or demand that we know of. It could be an abduction with a sexual motive, God forbid. It could be for another reason. Dita Olgweisch could have been killed accidentally. She could have been assisting the intruder. Or she could have been the primary target. How long had she worked for the Fullmans? DS Redman?"

Kate sat up straighter.

"Gemma Phillips says not long – two months. It seems to be Nick Fullman who employed her – I mean, it was at his request, rather than his wife's."

"Okay," said Anderton. "We'll need to talk to the Fullmans again, in much more detail. DS Olbeck, DS Redman, you'll accompany me on that trip. We'll go back this afternoon."

Kate watched. As Anderton talked, he had a habit of running his hands through his hair, tousling it roughly. For a man of fifty-plus, he had a good head of hair, grey as it was. He paced the confines of the crowded office and his team watched his every move. Kate was struck with the contrast of the last case in her previous job in Bournemouth, the murder of a middle-aged school teacher by her ex-husband. There, as the DCI had talked, her colleagues had surreptitiously checked their phones, whispered to one another, stared out of the window. Here, every eye was riveted on Anderton. Each officer sat alertly, even if leaning against their desks or straddling an office chair. *He has charisma*, she thought. *Damn.*

She dragged her attention back to what he was saying.

"Let's look into Olgweisch's background. Where did she come from, references, previous work history, does she have a boyfriend, etc, etc. Her parents have been informed and should be arriving from Poland in the next few days. They might be able to tell us more. What else?"

"The neighbours are being interviewed," said Olbeck. "As of yet, no one's seen anything of interest but it's early days."

"Fine. We'll need to collect statements from all the near neighbours, any other staff, the secretary and perhaps business associates of Nick Fullman." Anderton paused. "Do a bit of digging into his background, his business."

A DC with a head of vivid red curls raised her hand.

"Are the parents under suspicion, guv?" she asked.

There was no sound in the room, but Kate thought she could perceive a tightening of shoulders, a raised alertness in the people present. Anderton was silent for a moment. Then he spoke in a slow, deliberate tone.

"Everyone in that house – everyone with *access*

to that house – is under suspicion. That goes without saying. But I don't want anyone thinking that it's an open and shut case. It's not. We have no idea, at this stage, as to what happened. But." He paused and looked around the room, looking everyone in the eye, one by one. "I can't emphasise enough how delicately we must approach this. I don't want anyone steaming in and upsetting anyone with clumsy innuendo or their own prejudices. We take it very carefully. Do you understand me?"

"Yes sir," murmured Kate, part of the chorus.

"Good." He took his hand down from above his ear, releasing his hair. "Now everyone go and get some lunch. Redman, Olbeck, meet me back here at two. Thank you all."

He didn't exactly sweep from the room, but there was a sense, when the door shut behind him, that some huge surge of energy had dissipated. Kate turned to her new desk, blowing out her cheeks. All of a sudden, she felt exhausted. An unsatisfactory night's sleep due to new job nerves combined with the early morning start, the emotional maelstrom of the case, having to present the best side of herself to all her new colleagues... she fought the urge to put her head down on the keyboard and sleep.

"Canteen?" said Olbeck, appearing at her shoulder and making her jump.

"Sorry?"

"Fancy the canteen for lunch?"

Kate grinned tiredly. "Only if you can show me where it is."

"Hasn't anyone given you the tour yet?"

"Nope. But it doesn't matter. I pick things up pretty quickly."

Olbeck looked at her appraisingly. "I'm sure you do."

They began to walk towards the door. Kate made a mental note to introduce herself to the rest of the team when they got back, as no one had yet done that either.

WHEN THEY ARRIVED BACK AT the Fullmans' house that afternoon, Gemma Phillips opened the door to them. Her elaborate hairstyle was still immaculate, her make-up still a powdery mask across her face. She showed them through to a different room, a more formal type of living room that led off the cavernous hallway.

"Casey's lying down," she said after showing them in. "She took a tranquilliser and crashed out. She's totally out of it, I'm afraid."

"We will need to talk to her," said Anderton. "But perhaps Mr Fullman could come and see us in the meantime."

"He's on a conference call at the moment." She saw the look on their faces and said hurriedly, "But I can go and get him."

"A conference call!" said Kate as soon as Gemma had left the room. "What's the matter with the guy? His baby son has been abducted, his wife's prostrated, and he still has time to take a conference call?"

"Clearly–" said Anderton but could say nothing more as footsteps were heard coming back towards them through the hallway.

When Nick Fullman entered the room, Kate was reminded of two things. One, that he was very good looking. He had the cheekbones of a male model, the tall, muscular body of a professional athlete. His height and slimness were emphasised by the excellent cut of the expensive suit he wore. Two, she disliked him. Always one to examine her feelings, she acknowledged the emotion, held it up for examination. Why? He was insensitive and work-obsessed, yes. Was that the real reason? She didn't think so.

He was a fake, that was why. Working class origins hidden under a put-on accent and middle-class trappings. She couldn't have said how she knew that, but she did. *You know that you think that because you're just the same.* Kate took a deep breath and turned her attention back to the matter at hand.

Fullman took a seat in front of the large picture window. With the light behind him, it was difficult to clearly make out his expression. Was that deliberate? Did he really have something to hide? *Everyone's got something to hide, Kate.*

Anderton asked him about the sequences of events of the previous evening, taking him back through the hours before Charlie's disappearance and Dita's body were discovered. Fullman's story was unremarkable. He'd worked until nine o'clock the previous evening, the majority of it spent at the new development's offices in Wallingham. He'd then had a drink in a nearby bar with a friend, "a business acquaintance" as he'd put it, before returning home at eleven thirty.

"We'll need to talk to your business acquaintance," said Anderton. "Can your wife or someone else confirm the time you arrived home?"

Fullman looked wary.

"Dita opened the door to me. Casey was giving Charlie a bottle or something but she came out after she'd settled him and said goodnight."

"You didn't go to bed yourself?"

"Not for another hour or so. I had some work to do."

"A long day," said Anderton in a neutral tone. As if coppers knew nothing about long days or nights of work.

Fullman half smiled. "That's the way you make money."

Anderton nodded. "I can see that you're a

wealthy man, Mr Fullman. Do you think there's a possibility that your son has been kidnapped?"

"My God, I don't know."

"Has there been any ransom note? Any calls from people claiming to be holding your son?"

Fullman was shaking his head slowly. "No, no, nothing like that. Nothing at all." His phone rang suddenly, and he snatched at it, as if it were a reflexive action. After a second of staring at the screen, he pressed a button and the ringing stopped. "Sorry, what were you saying?"

"Have you received any suspicious calls? Any messages or notes or emails?"

"No. No, I don't think so." He went to the door and shouted. "Gemma! Come in here a second, would you?"

There was a quick tapping of high heels in the hallway outside, and Gemma Phillips put her head around the door. She looked flushed.

"Yes, Nick?"

"The police are asking if there's been any strange calls." He looked to Anderton as if for guidance. "About Charlie. Asking for a ransom."

Gemma's eyes widened.

"*Ransom* calls? Charlie's been *kidnapped*?"

"No, Miss Phillips," interjected Anderton quickly. "We're following up several lines of enquiry. Have there been any strange calls or messages that you're aware of?"

Gemma shook her head. She looked half appalled, half excited.

"No, nothing."

Nick Fullman sat down on one of the sofas abruptly and put his head in his hands. Gemma hesitated and crossed the room to sit down next to him and put her arms around him.

"I'm so sorry, Nick," she said, rocking him. Kate watched her closely. There was something slightly unsettling about her expression, something slightly too much of the cat that got the cream.

Kate cleared her throat. "Can I get your wife, sir? Do you need a moment?"

Nick looked up and then got up, dislodging Gemma's arms. She sat back, clearly trying to appear unruffled.

"I'm all right," he said. "This is just such a nightmare. I can't believe it's happening."

Anderton nodded.

"We won't keep you much longer, sir. Could you just tell me whether Charlie has a passport?"

Nick stared. "I don't know. I don't think so. He's only three months old."

"Of course, it's not very likely, but we just have to ascertain the facts. Would your wife know?"

Nick nodded and shrugged at the same time. He sat back down on the edge of the sofa, some feet away from Gemma, staring at the floor.

"I'll check," said Olbeck.

"No, don't worry," said Kate, quickly. "I'll talk to her."

Kate found the bedroom, knocked gently at the door, and then entered the room without waiting for an answer. Given what Gemma had said, she expected to find the woman inside fast asleep, but Casey was awake and sitting up. Kate sat on the edge of the bed; it was enormous, an acre of white linen and silk coverlet and scattered pillows.

Casey Fullman sat against the padded headboard, the sheets bunched and crumpled around her raised knees. She still looked like a child, something of the pallid Victorian waif of old-fashioned Christmas cards. She was hunched forward, her shoulders rounded, her hair tucked messily behind her ears. Every so often, she took a breath that was deeper, one that was almost a groan, as if a sudden pain caught her unawares every few minutes.

Kate, keeping her face blank, was wrenched with pity for this bereft mother. Someone who'd only been a mother three months. Was that all the motherhood she'd ever know? Kate took a deep, shaken breath, suddenly stabbed with pain herself. *Get a grip*. She sat up straighter and pushed, for the umpteenth time, those memories away. She reminded herself that, despite Casey's genuine distress, there was the possibility that she was somehow involved in her son's disappearance.

"Casey," she said gently. "This must be very distressing for you so I'm sorry to have to ask you, but I have a couple of questions."

Casey hunched her shoulders even more, pulling the duvet cover closer. "Okay."

"Are you able to talk for a few minutes?"

Casey sniffed and nodded.

"Firstly, could you tell me whether Charlie–" \

At the sound of his name, Casey groaned again.

Kate hurriedly went on. "Whether Charlie has a passport?"

Casey shook her head, wiping her hand under her nose. "No. No he doesn't." She started to cry again. "Oh, Charlie..."

"Casey, I'm sorry–"

The room was filled with the sound of sobbing. A few minutes passed, and Casey seemed to struggle to pull herself together. She took a few shuddering breaths.

"Sorry," she said eventually. "I'm okay now. I know you have to ask me things."

"Thank you," said Kate. She glanced down at her notes. "Can you just take me through what happened this morning, again?"

Casey kept her eyes downcast. Her long nails picked at a loose thread on the bed throw. "I woke up about eight o'clock. The light woke me. I knew something was wrong because it was too bright. I got up and went to see where Dita was with Charlie.

She normally wakes me up when he wants his first bottle." She stopped, cleared her throat. "I could see she wasn't in her room, so I went to Charlie's room and pushed open the door. I could see she was – she was – on the floor and her face was all – all wrong. And then I saw Charlie was missing."

"What happened then?"

Casey shot a quick look at her. "I screamed. I just kept screaming. I think Nick came running and he saw Dita – he shouted out something but I can't remember what – I just kept screaming for Charlie over and over again."

"What did you think had happened?"

"I don't know." Casey put a hand up to her eyes. "I wasn't thinking anything, I was just so upset, I couldn't stop screaming."

"Okay. What did Nick do?"

"Then?"

"Yes, immediately after he realised Charlie was missing – what did he do?"

"He got his phone and called the police, I think. He must have done."

"He did that straight away?"

"Yes. Yes, I think so."

Kate pulled her shoulders back, stretching out the ache in her neck. Casey's statement tallied with the one she'd given earlier. The time of the emergency call from the Fullman's house corresponded with the time Casey had given. It all seemed quite straightforward.

"You and Nick haven't been married long, have you?" asked Kate, changing tack.

Casey looked at her in surprise. "Almost a year. We got married last April."

"How did you meet?"

Casey almost smiled, her bunchy cheeks blossoming outwards. "At a party. I was in this TV show, and Nick came to the wrap party afterwards."

"That was the show about the hairdressers, wasn't it?"

"That's right. Did you see it?"

Kate would rather poke her own eyes out with a fork than watch any kind of reality TV show, but this was probably not the time to mention this. "Um, I think I may have seen it once or twice. I don't get time to watch much television, to be honest."

"Oh, right. Yeah, I guess so. Anyway, it was pretty big, lots of media attention, you know. I got quite a lot of work after it, modelling and that."

"Have you done much work lately? I don't suppose you've had time with Charlie being so young."

Casey's face clouded. "Not much. We did the *Okay* shoot after he was born. That was about the last thing." She pointed to the bedside cabinet. "There's a copy in there."

Kate retrieved the magazine. Casey took it from

her and leafed through it, fairly pointlessly, as the magazine quickly fell open at the required page. Kate guessed that the article had been looked at many, many times already. Casey handed it to her.

"Very nice," said Kate. She folded it up again, not wanting to see Charlie's little pink face in the photographs. "May I keep this?"

"Sure. We've got several copies."

I bet you have, thought Kate.

She began to gently question Casey again about her relationship with Nick, their first meeting, the quick progression of their romance, their marriage. From Casey's rather hesitant answers, she gathered that neither Nick nor Casey had been exactly footloose and fancy-free when they'd got together. Still, what could you expect from these sort of people – a Z-list model and a social climber? She inwardly grimaced as soon as the thought had crossed her mind. What was the matter with her? What had Anderton said? *I don't want anyone steaming in and upsetting anyone with clumsy innuendo or their own prejudices.*

There was a knock at the door and Anderton poked his head into the room.

"Mrs Fullman, I hope you're feeling better."

"Yes," said Casey, unhappily.

"We'll be off now, but we'll be in touch very soon. There'll be a family liaison officer staying behind to support you and of course, if there are any problems, don't hesitate to get in touch. DS Redman, could you come with me?"

"Of course, sir." Kate got off the bed. Casey clutched at her arm suddenly.

"Will you find him, find Charlie? *Please*."

Kate sat back down. "We're doing all we can, Mrs Fullman. I know it's hard to wait, but you must believe that we're doing absolutely everything we can."

Casey sagged back against the headboard. She was quiet for a moment and as Kate watched, her eyes filled with tears. She made no attempt to wipe them away and they trembled on the edge of her eyelids before sliding down her cheeks. She gasped. "Who could have taken him? I can't bear it. What if I never get him back?"

Kate leaned forward. She fought down the impulse to take Casey into her arms and rock her like the baby she was missing. "We'll get him back, Casey." She fixed the crying woman with her eyes. "We'll get him back for you."

I don't care what it takes, she added mentally.

IT WAS NINE THIRTY AT night by the time Kate unlocked her front door. She kicked off her shoes and considered collapsing face down in the hallway before deciding to at least make it to the sofa. She sat back against the cushions, dropping her head against the back of the couch. She was so tired that if she sat there for more than a minute, she would fall asleep.

After thirty seconds, she got up, got undressed and into her pyjamas and stood by the fridge, contemplating what was inside it with little enthusiasm. *Another ready-meal heated up, then.* She made herself a hot chocolate and cradled the cup in both hands, feeling the steam gently heat her face. So comforting, like a memory of childhood, although not *her* childhood. She picked up the phone, glancing at the clock. A bit late to call, although there was always a fighting chance that her mum would still be fairly sober. She dialled.

"Hello?"

"Mum, it's Kate."

"Who?"

"It's *Kate.*"

There was silence on the other end of the phone. Kate sighed and gave in. "It's Kelly."

"Oh, hello love. What you doing calling me so late?" Her mum's voice had a trace of a slur, nothing too bad yet. Perhaps she'd even remember her conversation with her eldest daughter in the morning. Kate never knew whether her mum genuinely forgot that she'd changed her name when she was eighteen, or whether her refusal to remember was a way of signalling her disapproval.

"Coppers treating you well, are they?" Mary Redman always said that.

"Fine, thanks Mum."

"So, what's up? Why you calling me so late?"

Kate was silent for a moment. Why *was* she calling? All of a sudden, she felt like crying.

"Just wanted to make sure you were all right," she managed, after a moment.

"I'm all right, love."

In the background, Kate heard the clink of a bottle as it chimed on the edge of the glass. She sighed again, inwardly. She really needed to get some sleep. "Well, it *is* late," she said. "I'll let you go, Mum. Sorry if I disturbed you."

"Come'n see me soon."

"Will do. Night night."

After she hung up, Kate drank the rest of her cooling chocolate. She had her second shower of the day, dropped her clothes into the laundry basket, cleaned her teeth and her face, patted in moisturiser. She made the last round of the night, checking everything was neat and ordered and clean and tidy. She set her alarm for the morning. There was something to be said for going to bed dead on your feet – it stopped you thinking so much.

In her bed, clean and ironed duvet cover drawn up to her face, she remembered Casey, marooned on her giant white bed. Her last thought was of the photographs of Charlie in *Okay* magazine, his little face wrapped in sleep, tiny fists clenched. *I'll find you*, she murmured.

Unconsciousness broke over her in a grey and smothering wave.

Chapter Four

THE POST-MORTEM OF DITA OLGWEISCH took place the next morning. Kate attended with Anderton, minus Olbeck who had the unenviable task of gently questioning Dita's grieving parents. The Olgweischs had arrived on the first available flight from Warsaw that morning. Kate was heartily glad not to have that particular job – watching a corpse being dissected and examined would be the easier option.

The pathologist was a young woman of almost ethereal fairness; her white-blond hair was drawn back severely from a central parting, a hairstyle which emphasised her wide forehead and long, narrow nose. With her pallor, her colouring and her extreme thinness, she looked a suitably macabre doctor of the dead. But Doctor Telling, despite her bizarre appearance, was deft and gentle in her examination, explaining her findings in a quiet, measured tone. Her skilled fingers had repaired some of the damage to Dita's face, and Kate was glad, knowing her parents would soon be seeing the body.

"The blow to the head is what killed her, as you can probably see," said Doctor Telling. "Someone swung something hard into her right temple. I'm not sure what yet. Whatever it was fractured her skull and caused severe traumatic damage. It would have been instantaneous."

"I'm assuming that it was a deliberate blow?" said Anderton.

"You would assume correctly. Of course, we can't possibly know that it was meant to kill. It could quite easily have been meant to disable. It's impossible to say."

Anderton raised his hand, hefting an invisible weapon.

"Kate, face me for a sec."

Kate hurried to comply, a little unnerved at how intimate it felt to be called by her first name. Anderton pretended to strike her across the face, quite slowly, stopping his hand about an inch from her face. He struck with one hand, then the other, forehand and backhand. Kate tried not to flinch and then tried not to smile. Doctor Telling watched them impassively, the shrouded body of Dita Olgweisch between her and the police officers.

"Hmm," said Anderton, eventually. He dropped his hand and nodded at Kate. "Thanks Kate. Well done, you'll live." Kate did smile at that. He looked at the pathologist. "Seems easy enough to do – to strike a hard blow, I mean, without trying hard."

"Easy enough for a strong man," said Doctor Telling.

"So a woman couldn't have done it?"

"No, either gender could do it, given enough force. It would just be easier for a man to – to overdo it accidentally, is what I meant."

"Right."

The traffic was heavy on the drive back to the station, and the car was stationary for minutes at a time. Kate found the silence between her and Anderton awkward, although she hoped that feeling wasn't mutual. She struggled to think of an appropriate topic of conversation, either case-related or small-talk line. She opened her mouth and shut it again. Anderton glanced over.

"We've thrown you in at the deep end with this one, DS Redman, haven't we?"

Kate smiled, a little uncomfortably. What happened to "Kate?"

"I've never worked a child abduction case before, sir, that's true."

"Always hard," said Anderton. "You never get used to the kid cases. Never." He indicated to turn right. "I've got three myself and you always find yourself thinking, well, what if it was one of mine?"

"Yes, I can see that."

"You don't have any kids yourself?"

Kate looked down at her hands folded in her lap. "No. No, I don't."

"Still hard," said Anderton, briefly. The police station car park gates were opening for them. Anderton swung the car into an empty bay.

Olbeck was shepherding a middle-aged couple through the foyer of the station as they came into the building. The couple looked bludgeoned, stunned into silence; the woman clutched her husband's arm as if it were the only thing keeping her from collapse. Kate and Anderton stood back, letting Olbeck steer the murdered girl's parents out towards his car, on their sad journey to view the mortal remains of their only daughter. Kate felt the first welcome surge of anger towards the perpetrator, the first real pulse of rage at whoever had done this; they had wrecked lives and shattered dreams for whatever selfish reason of their own.

They were approaching the front desk when Anderton was intercepted by a uniformed officer, who drew him aside and muttered something in his ear. Kate watched as Anderton raised his eyebrows. He looked over at her a second later and jerked his head to the right.

"Developments?" asked Kate, as they made their way down the corridor to the interview rooms.

"Certainly." Anderton stood back courteously, holding a door open for her. "We have a witness, apparently. Someone who saw something on the night of the abduction."

"Who is it?"

"A local wino, apparently. What makes it interesting, though," Anderton stood back again to let Kate go first and this time she felt a spasm of irritation. *Just get on with it*. "Our witness was once accused of sexual assault. No conviction, to be fair."

"And?" said Kate, stampeding ahead of him through the last doorway.

"The accusation was that he sexually assaulted an eighteen-month-old baby boy."

Kate stopped the door from swinging back into her superior's face. "Are you saying – what are you saying? Is he a suspect?"

"I don't know. All I'm saying is that we need to hear what he's got to say. It's probably nothing – but then again, it could be an extremely effective smokescreen."

They had reached the interview room. Kate reached out and lifted the flap that covered the peep-hole in the door. She could see the edge of the table, a leg clad in dirty denim, the edge of a filthy leather jacket.

"Why would someone like that draw attention to themselves?" she murmured, almost to herself.

"Good question."

Anderton put a hand on her arm and gently pushed her out of the way, opening the door. Kate felt herself beginning to blush. She forced the heat down by an extreme effort of will and entered the room with a face she felt was as blank as she could make it.

"For the tape, this is Detective Inspector Anderton interviewing Nicholas Draker, at two forty-nine pm, Monday sixteenth January 20—. Detective Sergeant Kate Redman is also present."

Nicholas Draker was younger than Kate had anticipated. He didn't look much more than forty-five, which, given his homelessness and general air of squalor, meant he was probably no more than thirty. He had a rounded face, long fair eyelashes and an upturned, piggish nose, all of which jarred with the greasy dark hair falling over his high forehead and the heavy stubble darkening his chin.

"So you admit to being on the grounds of Mr Fullman's estate on the night of Saturday the fourteenth of January, Mr Draker?"

"Yeah, I was there. I needed a place to kip."

"So in fact you were trespassing on Mr Fullman's land?"

Draker scoffed. "You can call it that if you want. Weren't doing any harm, was I?"

"Weren't you, Mr Draker? That remains to be seen." Anderton leant forward in his chair. "The Fullmans' baby son is missing, as well you know. A young woman has been killed. Did you have anything to do with these two events?"

"Course I fucking didn't."

"But you admit to being on the scene on the night of the crime?"

"I just said so, didn't I? Didn't mean that I had anything to do with it. I was there a week before all this happened and the night after it too. That's where I stay at the moment, or at least I did until you bastards moved me off. Where'm I going to go now?" No one answered him. "Look, I'm helping you out. I didn't need to say anything, did I? Fact is, I saw someone, like I told your man out there when they brought me in."

Anderton leant forward again.

"So what did you see, Mr Draker?"

"A man in a hood. Black hoody-type thing. He was walking towards the house."

"Did you see his face?"

"Nope. He was kind of side on, his back to me, you know."

"This was on Saturday night? What time exactly?"

"I dunno, exactly. Don't have a watch. But it was late, midnight or thereabouts." Draker put his hand up to his stubbled jaw and rubbed it. "He was moving kind of – dunno, kind of carefully. Watching where he put his feet, you know. That's kind of what drew my eye."

Anderton was silent for a moment and Kate took the opportunity."It was dark, Mr Draker. How could you see this man?"

Draker gave her a look of outrage.

"You saying you don't believe me?"

"Not at all. I just wanted to get the full picture. How clearly could you see this man?"

"Clear enough," said Draker, sulkily. "Look, when you live rough, you get used to the dark. I can see in the dark much better'n you can, you know? I'm telling you, I saw a man, a bloke in a black hoody, that night. He was walking towards the house, looked like he knew exactly where he was going."

He blew out his cheeks. "Fucking coppers. Why am I doing your job for you?"

"Yes, thank you, Mr Draker," said Anderton, not sounding upset in the slightest. He looked down at the file on the table as if checking a fact. "You have a police record yourself, don't you? The fact is that you yourself have been accused of the sexual assault of a child."

If they had expected Draker to look ashamed, or shocked, they were disappointed. He scoffed, sitting back in his chair and rolling his eyes.

"That was the ex-missus, that was, stirring up shit for me. There weren't no conviction, was there? It was *nothing*. It was that bitch trying to make trouble for me. If you think I've got anything to do with what happened to the baby that night, you're dead wrong, right?"

"CHARMING CHARACTER," SAID KATE AFTERWARDS, back in the office. "Do we believe him?"

Anderton was prowling before the whiteboards again. He stood before the picture of Dita Olgweisch spread-eagled out on the nursery carpet.

"Probably," he said. "I think his offence record is something of a red herring. Just because he was once accused of the abuse of a toddler doesn't mean he suddenly decided one day to bypass all the security, get past the CCTV, break into a stranger's house, kill the nanny and abduct a pretty much newborn baby. No, if there was an intruder, then it's someone who knew what they were doing, who knew the house."

Kate noted the emphasis. "*If*," she said, carefully.

Anderton glanced at her. "If," he confirmed.

Kate hesitated. "So, do we believe that Draker saw someone in the woods on the night of the crime?"

Anderton resumed his pacing. "Again, probably," he said. "He most probably did see someone. Was it someone intent on the crime, though? Could have been a poacher."

Kate raised her eyebrows. "Do we still get poachers, sir?"

Anderton shot her a quick glance.

"This *is* the country, DS Redman. Perhaps it was a dogger." Kate tried not to smile. Anderton went on. "Could have been another tramp. Perhaps

Draker even imagined it or conjured it out of a meths bottle."

Kate swung her office chair back and forth, tapping a pen on the edge of the desk.

"Sir," she said eventually. "I'd like to interview Casey Fullman again. And Gemma Phillips as well. Particularly Gemma. I think there's something..." She hesitated, unsure of what to she was trying to say. "I'm not sure but I think there may be something she's not telling us."

"Good. Get onto it. We need to see them – the Fullmans – anyway. Always important to support the parents in a case like this until we – well, until we know more."

"I'll go first thing tomorrow."

Olbeck returned from his visit to the coroner's office looking tired. He stopped by Kate's desk and perched himself on the corner of it.

"You knocking off soon?" he asked.

Kate nodded her affirmative.

"Fancy a drink?"

Kate blinked. She considered refusing as politely as possible – it was late, she was tired and she barely knew him – but after a second's consideration decided that she may as well. The last thing she wanted to do was start to foster a reputation of being completely standoffish and unfriendly with her new colleagues.

They walked a few streets to the "coppers' pub."
Kate knew there was one near every station – the
quietest, least conspicuous place where you could
sink copious amounts of alcohol was where you were
going to find the off duty men and women trying to
rejoin the real world after their shift. This pub –
The Queen's Head, how anonymous – was exactly
that: sticky carpet, a few old men at the bar, some
battered leather booths and no background music.

"Good God, is that all you want?" said Olbeck,
when she asked for an orange juice and lemonade.

Kate half smiled. She wasn't going to explain
that after a lifetime of watching her mother hop on
and off the wagon, the appeal of alcohol had long
since receded.

"I'm thirsty," she said, which would do as a sort
of half-truth. They took their drinks to one of the
booths.

"God, what a day," said Olbeck. He slugged half
his pint down in one go.

"How did it go with the Olgweischs?"

"About as well as you can imagine."

Kate grimaced.

"Dita did have a boyfriend," Olbeck continued.
"He's been out of the country for the last couple of
days. Bit of a shock for him when he came back,
poor bastard. Anyway, he's coming in tomorrow."

His phone, which he'd left on the table next to

his pint glass, started to vibrate. They both regarded it for a second.

"Don't you need to answer that?" said Kate, after a few moments.

Olbeck shook his head. "It'll keep. Anyway, how are you finding it? Everyone said hello yet?"

"Yes, not that I can remember any of their names, unfortunately."

"Theo is the handsome one, Jane's the redhead, Jerry's the old one and Rav is the whippersnapper." Olbeck grinned. "Does that help you?"

Kate pretended to write in her notebook. "Immensely, thanks."

She got them another drink. "What's Anderton like to work for?" she asked, sitting back down again.

Olbeck took a sip of his pint. She got the impression he was picking the words of his answer carefully. Was that because of loyalty – or something else?

"He's steady," he said eventually. "Once he's got your back, he's got it for life, so to speak. But he doesn't suffer fools gladly. He's got his own way of doing things, and it doesn't always go down too well with the high-ups." Kate nodded. Olbeck continued. "He can be...what's the right word? Hard. Ruthless, maybe. You don't want to get on the wrong side of him."

Olbeck's phone rang again. With a suppressed

sigh, he picked it up. Kate got the impression that this was something of a recurring argument.

"No, I won't be late. It's just a quick drink." A pause. "With our new DS. Yes, I will. Yes. No, I won't." Kate caught his eye and he mimed a throat-cutting gesture with one hand. "No, I won't. Yes, all right. Sounds good. See you soon."

He cut off the call and placed the phone back on the table.

"Trouble?" said Kate.

"Just my other half." He didn't volunteer any more details.

"Do you need to go?"

"Yes, but I'm not going to. Have another drink?"

Kate didn't want to be the cause of any domestic strife. Besides, she had stuff to do and honour had been served with two drinks. She shook her head, trying to sound regretful.

"I'll pick you up in the morning," said Olbeck. "We're going back to the Fullmans' place with Anderton."

"Thanks for the drink."

"My pleasure."

Chapter Five

THERE WAS A SMALL CROWD outside the gates of the Fullmans' house when the officers arrived back the next morning. Kate thought they were curious onlookers until she spotted the cameras. Clearly the story had broken, and now the paparazzi were staking out the house, hoping to get a glimpse of the distraught parents.

"Vultures," said Olbeck, echoing Kate's thoughts. As they drove carefully through the gates, a fusillade of flashes went off. Kate turned her head away from the window. How anyone would want to be famous and actually *seek out* this kind of crap was a total and utter mystery. Inevitably, her thoughts turned to Casey. How was she coping?

As they drew up outside the house, she caught a glimpse of movement in one of the front rooms, the one they'd interviewed Nick Fullman in yesterday. She watched as Anderton parked the car. It was Nick with his arms wrapped around this wife, his dark head bent down to her blonde one. He seemed to be rocking her back and forth. Kate frowned. There was nothing more natural than a man in his situation comforting his wife but...well, she'd got the impression yesterday that he was not an affectionate man, not one to be patient and loving and kind. Perhaps she was wrong. She hoped she was.

Her first glimpse of Casey up close almost shocked her. The woman's skin was grey, her pupils huge and dilated. Her long hair hung in matted clumps. What was worse was her look of desperate hope.

"You've found him?" she gasped as the officers came into the hallway. She sagged as Anderton began to explain that they hadn't, that he was so sorry. Nick Fullman caught her and picked her up bodily.

"I'll take her into the bedroom," he said over his shoulder as he walked away with Casey sobbing in his arms. "Go into the kitchen and I'll be with you in a minute."

There was an older woman already in the kitchen, sat at the table with a steaming mug in front of her, flipping though a magazine. She was so like Casey, so much an older, more brittle copy of her daughter that Anderton didn't even bother to ask. He merely said, "You must be Casey's mother," and introduced himself and his team.

"Pleased to meet you," said Sheila Bright,

shaking hands with them all with a vigour that belied her tiny frame. She wasn't as old as Kate had thought – either that, or she'd had plastic surgery. Probably the latter, thought Kate. The apple doesn't fall far from the tree. Then she castigated herself for being a bitch. What did it matter anyway?

Gemma Phillips was also there, typing furiously into a laptop at the other end of the table. She was fully made up, dressed today in a light grey suit. Plain or not, she had an excellent figure, and it was clearly on show in her tight pencil skirt and fitted jacket. Kate frowned. There was something inappropriate about her dress, given the circumstances. But perhaps it was the only kind of wardrobe she had.

Nick Fullman had come back into the kitchen. He took a kitchen chair and swung it backwards, straddling it. There was something about the gesture that was a little familiar, and it took Kate only a few moments to realise that she'd seen Anderton do the same in the staff room just yesterday. Fullman had the same quality of dynamism, a palpable energy that seemed to radiate from him. Gemma Phillips was watching him intently. *She fancies him*, thought Kate, and knew she was right. She must talk to her again; it could be important.

Anderton was talking.

"Mr Fullman, we're doing all we can to find your son. I know we've ascertained that Charlie didn't have a passport, but we've still alerted all of the airports and ports. We've interviewed the neighbours to see if they can give us any information that might be helpful."

"And have they?"

"We're still going through their statements at this time but I have to say that nothing has particularly stuck out as suspicious." Kate wondered whether he would mention Nicholas Draker and what he had or hadn't seen. Anderton didn't. "Is there anything else that you might be able to tell us that might be pertinent to this enquiry?"

Nick Fullman frowned. "No. I don't think so."

Anderton changed tack.

"The other thing we're coming up against, sir, is the fact that none of the alarms on your property were activated last night."

Fullman blinked, as if this had only just occurred to him.

"They weren't?" He seemed to recollect himself. "No, of course they weren't. My God, I hadn't realised, I didn't think of it."

"Do you change the codes for the alarms often? How many alarms are there?"

Nick got up from his chair.

"There's only two alarms. One for the garage, one for the house."

"Do you change the codes often?"

Fullman looked a bit sheepish. "No, I don't think I've ever changed them. It's the same code for both."

"Who would know the alarm codes?"

Fullman was pacing up and down, clutching his mobile phone like a talisman. He didn't appear to have heard the question.

Anderton prompted him.

"Mr Fullman?"

He came to with a start. "Sorry, I was – sorry. Um, Casey and I know them, Dita, Gemma..."

"I do, love," said Mrs Bright. Nick turned to stare at her.

"Yes, you do too," he said.

"Anyone else?"

"I don't know..." Fullman stared out of the window at the leafless trees and frosty lawn of the garden. "We've had cleaners and gardeners and so on. I guess they might have had them... I don't know."

Olbeck and Kate glanced at each other. Anderton said, with a touch of severity, "I'll need a list of everyone who might have had access to the alarm codes, sir. Especially if you've never changed them. Can you do that for us straightaway?"

Gemma sat up in her chair.

"I can do that for you, Nick, don't worry," she said. Nick glanced at her and nodded slightly. He went back to staring out of the window. Anderton's slight admonishment apparently barely registered.

DITA OLGWEISCH'S BOYFRIEND, TOM SPENCER, was a twenty-something young man with a pleasant freckled face and a thatch of thick brown hair. He worked as an IT consultant and had been working in Frankfurt when Dita died. Olbeck and Kate interviewed him in one of the more pleasant rooms on the first floor of the station.

"I can't believe it, I just can't," he kept saying. A cup of cooling tea sat untouched before him. "It just doesn't seem possible. Dita was the last person..."

Olbeck murmured something about being sorry for his loss and then asked whether Dita had enjoyed her job.

"She thought it was okay. I mean, it was just a stopgap. She was just doing it to earn some money. She'd done some work in a nursery back in Warsaw, while she was at university, and so I guess that's why they took her on. She had experience. But it wasn't her *career*. She wanted to go back to studying. She wants to be an architect. Wanted, I mean." His voice shook for a moment and he cleared his throat.

"Did she like her employers?"

Tom looked uneasy. "Well, I suppose so. They were okay."

"Only okay? Can you elaborate?"

"Well, I got the impression that the mother – that's Casey – didn't really want Dita there. So she could be a bit – a bit standoffish, I suppose. Dita always said she was really touchy about anyone else picking Charlie up while she – Casey, I mean – was in the room. If he cried."

"So, from what Dita said, Casey didn't really want a nanny? It was all Mr Fullman's idea?"

Tom nodded. "That's right. He had Dita start before the baby was even born, just helping out with housework and stuff."

Olbeck looked at Kate. She nodded very slightly.

"Do you know if Mr Fullman ever, well, looked after his child? Did he ever take over the care of Charlie when Dita or Casey wasn't there?"

Tom looked mystified. "I don't think so. I don't know."

Kate paused for a moment.

"Did Dita ever mention anyone who'd ever made any threats to the Fullmans? Any strange notes or incidents?"

"Threats?"

"Well, anything that might be construed as a threat. Anything out of the ordinary."

Tom looked down at the table. Kate didn't push him; she could see he was thinking deeply.

"There was one thing," he said eventually. Olbeck nodded encouragingly. "A guy came to the door one time. An Asian guy in a flash car. Dita knew because she'd opened the door to him. Casey came out and took him into one of the rooms, and they had a huge argument. Shouting and screaming and all that."

"Really? What were they arguing about?"

"I'm not sure. Dita took Charlie away because he was getting upset because of the noise. It's just that afterwards, Casey asked her not to mention it to Nick."

"Mrs Fullman didn't want her husband to know about this?"

"That's right. That's what Dita said."

"When was this?"

"Not that long ago. Maybe a month? I remember because we actually saw the guy again, Dita and me." Tom brushed back a lock of hair that had fallen over his broad forehead. "We were out having dinner in Wallingham, and Dita saw him, pointed him out to me. She said, 'There's that man, the one that Casey had such a fight with. The secret one, the one I couldn't tell about.' I remember because he was getting out of his car, and it was a *nice* car, an Audi RS."

Kate tapped her fingers on the edge of the table. "Did this man ever come to the house again?"

Tom shrugged. "If he did, Dita didn't see him."

They watched Tom walk away down the street from the window of the incident room on the second floor.

"Poor bugger," said Olbeck.

"Mmm." Kate put a hand up to her head, checking the neatness of her ponytail. She tucked in an errant wisp. "So who is the mystery man and is it important?"

"We'll have to ask Casey Fullman."

"But not in front of her husband."

"Good point," said Olbeck. "Not right now, anyway. How about a bit of lunch?"

Kate grinned. "Are you *always* hungry?"

For a moment, she wondered whether it was a bit too early on in their professional relationship for teasing. Luckily, Olbeck was smiling.

"You sound just like Joe," he said. "Always nagging me about my weight."

"I wasn't!"

"Teasing."

"Oh." Kate paused a moment, flustered. "Is Jo your partner?"

"That's right." There was a brief moment of silence. "Anyway, now we've established that I'm a greedy bugger, can we go and get some lunch?"

They were coming back from the canteen when they spotted Theo waving at them across the incident room.

"We've got something on the CCTV," he said. "The same car, seen in the vicinity of the house several times over the past two weeks. Pretty flashy car, it's an–"

"Audi RS?" said Olbeck.

Theo gasped. "That's right. You've seen the footage?"

"Not yet." Olbeck leaned over Theo's desk. "Let's see."

They all watched the grainy footage of the road outside the Fullmans' house, the flickering image of a powerful car moving slowly along, its headlights dimmed. Once, twice. Parked across from the gates for several minutes before moving off with a wheel spin. Driving past once more.

"It's definitely the same car," said Theo. His slim brown fingers manipulated the keyboard, bringing the image of the number plate up in close-up. "Whoever's driving it isn't making much of an effort to be discreet."

"What date was this?" said Kate. "Or dates?"

"I'll check. Give me five minutes."

"Run the plate number too, please."

Theo began to access the various databases needed for the information. Olbeck muttered something about getting hold of Anderton and walked off. Kate waited, holding each elbow in the opposite hand, tapping her foot. *Don't get too excited, Kate, it's probably nothing.*

"Here we go," said Theo after a few minutes. "Car's registered to an Ali Saheed, 15 Canterbury Mansion, London, SW7." He handed Kate the piece of paper he'd scribbled the details down on.

"Thanks." She looked down at the address. SW7 was Knightsbridge, wasn't it? Somewhere like that.

Olbeck had returned. Kate showed him their find.

"Anderton said we've got to talk to Casey and follow up this lead." He looked at the address. "South Ken. Hmm."

"I'll talk to Casey," said Kate.

There were even more photographers outside the Fullmans' gate this time. Kate had to edge forward carefully, tapping her horn once or twice as the gates slowly swung open. She was almost immune to the flashes of the cameras by now and kept her face neutral, not blinking or showing any kind of emotion.

Casey opened the door to her. She was wearing the same clothes she'd had on yesterday: expensive lounge wear marked with what looked to be splashes of tea, smudges of makeup, other unidentifiable stains. Her soft, rounded face seemed to be growing thinner by the day.

"Is Mr Fullman in?" asked Kate as they made their way through the house to the kitchen.

Casey shook her head. "He and Gemma had to go out, they had a meeting."

Kate inwardly chastised him, but she was also thankful. She wanted to talk to Casey alone.

Casey stood in the middle of the kitchen floor. She looked a little lost, awkward, as if it wasn't her kitchen after all. Kate thought back to Gemma

Phillips making tea for them all on that first day, of
how much more at home she had seemed.

"Do you want a drink or something?" said Casey.

"No, thank you." Kate watched without comment
as Casey poured herself a glass of wine. It was
only three o'clock in the afternoon. But if anyone
needed a drink, it was this poor girl. *Woman, Kate,
woman*. It was hard to think of Casey as a woman;
she was so tiny and somehow undeveloped, despite
the artificial curves. It was hard to think of her as
a mother.

"You might remember that we asked your
husband whether anyone had made any threats
against you, or whether there had been any strange
occurrences or anything like that happening." Casey
half nodded, her eyes cast down and her hands
clasped around her wine glass. "Has anything come
to mind?"

"No."

"Nothing at all?

"No. Not that I can think of," said Casey.

Kate tapped her fingers on her leg. "It's just that
we've been told that you had something of an – an
altercation with a man recently. Someone came to
the house and you had a – well, had a bit of a row?"

Casey looked up.

"No. I don't remember that."

"He was described as an Asian man." Kate
persisted. Then, thinking of the name, "Perhaps

Middle Eastern might be more accurate. Apparently this happened fairly recently." She didn't want to say the name aloud – she wanted Casey to say it. If it were true.

"Who told you that?" said Casey. She frowned. "I bet it was Gemma."

"I can't tell you that, Mrs Fullman, I'm sorry. Is it true?"

Casey didn't seem to have heard her. "She'd say anything to get me into trouble," she muttered, seemingly to herself. She was staring off into the middle distance.

"Was there a row with this man?" said Kate doggedly.

Casey appeared to come back to reality. She slid a sideways glance at Kate. "It wasn't really a row. Just a – a difference of opinion."

"Who is this man?"

Casey slugged back the remains of her wine.

"It was only Ali. That's all. No one – no one sinister."

"Who is Ali?"

"He's my agent. Former agent. We decided to go our separate ways. That's all. He was probably just a bit pissed off at something. It can't have anything to do with this." Her eyes filled. "He wouldn't have had anything to do with this. He *couldn't* have."

"Who can't have?"

Kate and Casey both jumped. Nick Fullman had

come into the kitchen unnoticed by both of them. Kate was struck once again by his male-model looks and something she hadn't really grasped before, the sense of physical power he exuded. Casey seemed to shrink back into herself as he came closer.

"Nothing," she said, her voice shaking. "Nothing, Nick."

"What were you talking about?"

He was looming over both women, sat as they were on one of the sofas. Kate stood up quickly and stepped forward into his personal space, forcing him to take a step back.

"I was just questioning your wife about a car that had been seen in the vicinity recently," she said pleasantly. Nick raised his eyebrows.

"What car?"

Kate was silent for a moment, wondering whether to bring forward the subject of her conversation with Casey. Casey solved her dilemma.

"Just Ali's car, Nick, that's all," she said. She turned to put her empty glass down on the nearest side table and knocked it over, catching it before it rolled onto the floor. "You know, when he came to drop that stuff back. That's all."

Nick frowned.

"You think he's got something to do with this? That little shit?"

"We're following several lines of enquiry, sir,"

said Kate smoothly. Nick sat down at the table and put his head in his hands.

"This whole thing is just a nightmare," he said in a muffled voice. The two women watched him. He raised his head again and there were tears in his eyes.

"I keep thinking I'm going to wake up and it'll all be over," he said. He dropped his head back down. "It just keeps going on and on."

Casey jumped up and flung her arms around him. Kate stood for a moment, watching the embracing couple. I should feel sympathetic for him, she thought. But I don't. Why don't I? Is it because I think he's just saying something for the sake of it, that he doesn't really mean it after all? Am I getting that hard, that cynical – or is there something in what I'm thinking?

Chapter Six

Olbeck and Theo had driven to Ali Saheed's flat in South Kensington, fully expecting to find him away as it was the middle of a normal working day. Olbeck had queried whether they could have gotten a search warrant, but he knew that the process would involve several hours of form filling and sign offs. He was impatient to chase up this latest lead, even if it meant time wasted in trying to track down their latest suspect.

Saheed's flat was a basement one, in a street just off the Brompton Road. The elegant, white Georgian townhouses stood in serried rows, painted black railings separating them. The basement forecourt of the flat was empty, save for a solitary bay tree in a large stone pot standing like a sentinel by the front door. Olbeck rang the bell, not expecting an answer, but to their surprise, they heard footsteps approaching the door before it swung open.

The man regarding them with suspicion was short, although powerfully built, with carefully-tousled, thick black hair. He wore a suit that Olbeck's practised eye picked out as an Oswald Boteng and, rather jarringly, bare feet.

"Yeah?"

"Ali Saheed?" said Theo.

"Yeah," said Saheed, more warily. "What's this about?"

"Charlie Fullman, Mr Saheed," said Olbeck. "Mind if we come in?"

The flat was small but luxuriously furnished: granite-topped kitchen counters, black gloss units, black leather sofas and an enormous flat screen television. An empty espresso cup stood on the glass-topped coffee table, along with a packet of Silk Cut, a lighter and an ash-filled glass ashtray.

"I heard about the baby," said Saheed, who perched himself on the edge of one of the sofas, as if he was about to spring up at any time. "And that poor girl. It's terrible. I tried to give Casey a ring but–"

"Yes, Casey Fullman," said Olbeck. "I understand that you are her former agent?"

"Yeah."

"When did you – part company?"

Saheed reached for his cigarettes. "Not sure. Not long ago. Maybe a couple of months."

"So just after Charlie Fullman was born, really. Is that right?"

Saheed shrugged. "I guess so."

Olbeck leant forward. "Now we've been told that you and she had something of a fight recently, is that right?"

"A fight?" said Saheed. He looked uncomfortable. "No, not really, just a – well, a disagreement. That's all."

"What was the disagreement about?"

"Oh, nothing," said Saheed. He must have realised that that didn't satisfy them, as he went on, "I just thought she was making a mistake, that's all. About sacking me as her agent. I thought – I thought she was doing it for the wrong reasons, that's all. I just wanted to talk to her about it."

"What were her reasons?"

Saheed had smoked his cigarette down to the filter. He crushed it out in the ashtray with disproportionate violence.

"That's confidential."

"Nothing's confidential in a murder case, Mr Saheed."

Saheed looked startled. Olbeck wondered if he was unused to being told no in any form. But as a theatrical agent, surely he heard it all the time? That was Joe's department, that sort of world. Olbeck resolved to try and get home at a normal sort of time, if he could, to try and talk to his partner about the industry.

"Her reasons, Mr Saheed?" he prompted.

Saheed shrugged.

"She – she just thought that I wasn't helping her enough. Wasn't getting her enough work. She'd just had a baby, for Christ's sake, she shouldn't have been thinking about work. She wasn't thinking straight."

Olbeck had been looking unobtrusively around the flat as they spoke. He didn't really think there would be any trace of anything belonging to Charlie Fullman, certainly not left in plain sight if Saheed had in fact taken him – and Olbeck was far from convinced that was the case – but you never knew. There was nothing to be seen, anyway, nothing but the usual detritus of a bachelor pad. His house had once looked something like this. No longer, since Joe had moved in. He sighed, inwardly.

"So this fight, my apologies, this disagreement you had with Mrs Fullman...was that the only time you'd been to their house in recent weeks?"

Saheed had lit another cigarette. Sheets of bluish smoke hung in the air, and Theo smothered a cough.

"That's right," said Saheed.

"That was the only time?"

"Yeah."

"You're quite sure about that, are you?" said Olbeck, holding his gaze. Saheed gazed back angrily.

"I said, *yes*. That's the only time."

Theo and Olbeck exchanged a glance.

"Well, Mr Saheed, I'm afraid that I don't quite believe you. Your very distinctive car has been seen on numerous occasions on the road outside the Fullmans' house, both driving past and parked on the verge. What were you doing there?"

The hand holding the cigarette was shaking.

"Nothing, I..." said Saheed. He dropped his eyes to the floor. "I wasn't doing any harm. Just parked on the road. That's not being at the house, is it?" He looked at them fearfully. "I had nothing to do with this, nothing, I'm telling you." The policemen regarded him with impassive faces. He swallowed. "Do I need a lawyer?"

He accompanied them back to the station with Theo sitting next to him in the back seat of the car. The traffic was heavy, and the journey took an hour longer than it had taken to get there. Olbeck thought of Kate and wondered how she was getting on at the Fullmans' house, questioning Casey.

Back at the station, they took Saheed into an interview room, accompanied by the duty solicitor.

"I'm telling you, I don't know anything about this," he kept saying. "All right, so I drove by a few times. I kept thinking that Casey would–" He was silent for a moment. "That Casey would change her mind."

"About employing you again as her agent?" said Theo.

Saheed nodded, after a moment.

"I'm assuming that she didn't, in fact, do this?"

Saheed's black brows drew down in a frown. "I'd been with her for five years," he said. "Five years. I got her that TV show, I got her into the papers. Five years and she just throws me away, bye-bye Ali, nice to have known you."

"That must have rankled," said Olbeck, non-committedly.

"Yeah," said Saheed, a trifle uncertainly. Olbeck wondered whether he knew what rankled actually meant. "I was pretty pissed off."

"So pissed off that you thought you'd do something drastic? Something to get back at her?"

Saheed stared at him. "No. Nothing like that. I told you, I had nothing to do with Charlie going missing – and the nanny – nothing to do with it. You've got to believe me."

"So why were you driving up and down outside her house at all hours of the day and night?"

"I was – I was thinking." Olbeck looked sceptical. "All right, I was thinking about going back to see her. To try and persuade her to change her mind."

Olbeck sat back in his chair. Perhaps it was time to try another tack.

"What was your relationship with Mr Fullman like?"

Saheed stared again. "Like?"

"Did you get on well? How did he feel about your relationship with his wife?"

"Okay, I guess." There was a short silence. "He's a weird guy, you know. He's totally obsessed with his work, that's all he thinks about. Casey got fed up with it, sometimes."

"So Mrs Fullman would confide in you? You were close friends as well as business associates?"

Saheed half smiled. "I guess. You do get close, you know – when you both know the game..." He dropped his head. "She was lonely."

Theo and Olbeck exchanged a glance.

"So you're saying that, perhaps the Fullmans' marriage was in trouble? Under strain?"

Saheed shrugged.

"For the tape, please."

"What? Oh–" Saheed glanced over at the recorder. "I don't know what their marriage was like, we didn't really talk like *that*. Casey just used to say that Nick was always working and it pissed her off sometimes, particularly after she got pregnant. He didn't seem very excited about the baby. That's what I remember her saying, he didn't seem excited at all about the baby, and he was the one who'd suggested the whole thing to her."

Olbeck raised his eyebrows. "Nick Fullman suggested what to his wife?"

"That they have the baby, you know. Casey's still young, you know, she's not twenty seven yet. She's got loads of time to have a baby if she wanted one. Nick was the one who was keen to have one."

"Is that right? But Mrs Fullman took some persuading?"

"No, Casey wanted kids as well, it's just that – oh, I dunno – it was more that she would have waited..."

"Do you think the Fullmans are happily married?"

Saheed's eyebrows went up. "I don't know."

"What is your opinion?"

He looked uncomfortable. "I don't know. Maybe."

"You said Mr Fullman is a 'weird guy'. Can you explain any further?"

Saheed reached for his cigarettes and then realised that he wasn't going to be able to smoke. His foot was jiggling up and down on the floor and he put a hand on his knee, obviously to stop it.

"Don't know," he said. "All I know is that Nick does what he wants all the time. It's always about him. He gets his own way a lot of the time, seems to me. He always gets what he wants. One way or the other."

OLBECK GOT HOME LATER THAN he'd expected, and unfortunately, about two hours later than he'd promised. As he put the key in his front door, he braced himself. Joe was such a tempest, sometimes. There'd be storms of tears, shouting, even the odd plate thrown now and again. Then, just as quickly, calm again, all the energy dissipated. Olbeck knew he didn't deal with it very well. He'd tried being placatory and unruffled as he was berated for his wrongs, both real and imaginary. He'd tried shouting back. He hadn't thrown anything yet, but it was sometimes a near thing. It was *exhausting*, this relationship business, a constant battle between the compromises demanded by Joe and his own, selfish inclinations.

Joe was in the kitchen, clattering about with pots and pans. A rich, garlicky smell hung in the air, reminding Olbeck of the length of time that had passed since he'd last eaten. Joe was a fantastic cook; it was one of the things Olbeck loved about him.

"You're late," said Joe, not looking around.

"I know." Olbeck hesitated and then wrapped his arms around his partner, kissing the back of his neck. "You know how it is when I'm on a case. I'm sorry."

"You're always on a case. You *are* a case. Headcase."

"Nutcase."

"That too." Sighing petulantly, Joe turned around and kissed him properly. Despite his hunger and his tiredness, Olbeck felt a stir of interest. His boyfriend really was very nice looking, after all...

Then Joe moved away from him, stomping to the fridge. Olbeck sighed. Play this wrong, and it wouldn't only be separate beds tonight, he'd been lucky not to be wearing his dinner. *Be nice, be calm, be interested...* Trouble is, he didn't *want* to be interested. What he wanted to do was have a quick and dirty shag, something to eat and then hit the sack without any more conversation whatsoever.

"Guess what?" said Joe, in a slightly-less-annoyed tone. He was stirring a bubbling pot on the stove, bringing the spoon to his lips to taste. "Ouch, hot. Anyway, guess what?"

"What?"

"Mandy and Sarah are getting married. Well, civil partnership, you know."

"Oh right," said Olbeck, scrolling frantically through his mental contact list to try and place Mandy and Sarah. He remembered – Mandy was an actress friend of Joe's and Sarah was her girlfriend. "That's nice."

"Isn't it? They're such a fabulous couple. I bet they'll do the big white wedding thing, that's Mandy's style at least."

"Right," said Olbeck, trying not to yawn.

Joe glanced sideways at him. "That's the kind of thing I'd like, as well."

"What is?"

"The big white wedding."

Olbeck's heart sank. "Okay," he said, not really sure where this was going but not liking the sound of it.

"Don't you want that?"

No, I don't. Olbeck knew he couldn't say that out loud. Instead he muttered something like "Of course, but it's not the right time at the moment..."

Joe was pouting. "You could at least sound a bit more enthusiastic."

"Do we have to talk about this now? I'm tired and it's been a long day."

"No," said Joe, ominously quietly. "We don't have to talk about this now. God forbid that you want to *talk* about making a commitment to your partner, God forbid that I might actually want to talk to you for a change instead of getting your voicemail all the fucking *time*." His voice began to rise. "God forbid that I've been here all day cooking for you and you promised to get home on time, promised and yet a-fucking-gain you don't!"

"Okay–" said Olbeck, trying to head off the inevitable, but it was too late.

"I'm fucking sick of it!"

The wooden spoon went flying across the kitchen, trailing drips of sauce. Seconds later, Joe slammed out of the kitchen and Olbeck heard his footsteps pound up the stairs and then the more distant slam of the bedroom door.

Olbeck remained standing for a moment with his eyes shut, breathing deeply. Then he got himself a plate from the cupboard and helped himself to the stew. He sat at the table, eating methodically, refusing to get upset. Joe would calm down. Merely a storm in a tea-cup. The stew was so good he had second helpings before he stacked the plate into the dishwasher – there, who could say he never did anything around the house? – and went through to the front room to watch television.

Chapter Seven

KATE PARKED THE CAR IN her usual spot, four doors down from her mother's house. She sat for a moment, ostensibly checking her handbag for various items but actually steadying herself with some deep breaths. Being here brought back so many memories.

She stared at the shabby grass verge, the litter piled in the gutter, the mean little front gardens that were either littered with garish plastic toys or paved over to become parking spaces. The houses were the usual charmless 1960s square boxes: windows slightly too small for the walls, concrete roof tiles, white plastic cladding.

Looking around, Kate realised the area had actually improved slightly – clearly, most of these houses were now privately owned including, incredibly, her mother's home. Kate had given her the deposit to enable her to take advantage of the Right to Buy scheme back in the mid nineties. Kate had delayed her own house purchase by a few years because she gave up that chunk of hard-earned savings. Now, looking at the peeling paint, the cracked window pane, the overgrown front garden, Kate thought she might as well have thrown that money down the toilet. *Loo, Kate, loo*. At least if her mum's property was still council-owned, it would be in better shape. She straightened her shoulders, locked the car and went up to the front door. She had timed this visit carefully. Too early, and her mum would be hungover and grumpy and unwelcoming, too late, and she'd be half-cut and sloppily sentimental. Now, at half past two in the afternoon, Mrs Redman would be as rational and as normal as she could be. So Kate hoped.

She was halfway to the front door when it opened violently and someone came stampeding out, her mother's screamed profanities following them. Kate flinched. The person running down the path was a teenage girl, hair teased up into a beehive, thick black eyeliner, stomping boots on the end of long legs. She pushed past Kate, scowling murderously. Kate's mother stood at the door, screaming after her. "And don't come back, you little whore!"

"Mum!" said Kate. She grabbed her mother's arm and wheeled her around, pushing her back into the house. She was rocketed back to her teenage years, feeling the neighbours' scorn and disapproval beaming out from the surrounding houses as her mum embarrassed her yet again. "What on earth? What's going on? Who was that?"

Her mum looked at her with a disbelieving expression.

"What d'you mean, who was that? That was *Courtney*, wasn't it? Little whore. Who'd she think she is, coming round here and trying to hit me up for cash?"

Kate felt a quick jab of shame. Courtney was one of her six half-siblings. Her own sister, and she hadn't even recognised her. When had she last seen her? Over a year ago, at least.

"Oh," she said feebly. Then, collecting herself, "Well, Mum, here I am."

"Yeah."

"I was going to ask what's been going on but I see that plenty has."

Her mother tottered off into the messy living room.

"Where's my fags?" she muttered, hunting amongst the detritus of the coffee table.

"How about a cup of tea?" said Kate. She wanted to deflect the inevitable offering of "a glass of something."

Mary Redman had found her cigarettes and lit one. A thin ribbon of smoke rose towards the ceiling, stained ochre by twenty year's worth of exhaled fumes. Kate turned towards the tiny galley kitchen that lay at the end of the hallway.

She hunted for teabags and mugs amongst the chaos. Mary leant against the doorframe, watching her.

"*That* cupboard," she said, eventually. Kate opened it and was nearly brained by a landslide of tins and cardboard boxes.

"Oh, leave it," said Mary, as Kate scrabbled about on the floor, picking things up. "What's up with you, then? What you been up to?"

Kate stood up. She mentioned the Fullman case, just the bare bones of it, all she was able to say.

"Awful," said Mary, taking a long drag. She shook her head. "Don't know what I would have done if one of you had been taken. And that poor girl with her head smashed in!" Kate winced. "Poor little baby. His mum must be frantic."

Kate poured boiling water onto the teabags and nodded. She thought of Casey in her expensive prison, hemmed in by paparazzi, lost and alone in her glossy kitchen. A greater contrast to the one that she was in could scarcely be imagined.

"Here you go," she said, handing her mother a steaming mug.

Mary placed it precariously on the counter.

"Surprised you're doing this case," she said, watching Kate closely. "Thought it might bring back a few bad memories."

Kate felt her shoulders stiffen. "I don't know what you mean," she said.

"Don't you?" said Mary.

"No," said Kate. She could hear it in her voice: the shut-down, the freezing of emotion.

There was a moment's silence.

"Oh, well," said Mary. She picked up her tea and turned away. "Don't know how you did it, myself. That was proper cold, Kelly, it weren't natural. Couldn't have done it myself. Don't know how you–"

"*That's enough.*"

Kate's voice made them both jump. She stood for a moment, breathing deeply, trembling, trying to keep herself together. Her mother was looking at her in an odd way, sympathy and spite mixed together.

"Want a glass of something?" said Mary, after a moment.

"No thanks," said Kate, automatically. She looked out of the small kitchen window into the uninspiring garden: concrete paving slabs, a dying shrub in a pot, a handkerchief-sized, balding lawn. There was a white plastic table out there, with an empty whisky bottle on top of it, an inch of dirty water in the bottom of the bottle.

"What did Courtney want?" she asked, after a moment.

Mary sniffed. "Money. As usual. As if she don't already get enough from her dad."

"But is she okay?"

"'Course she is. Just being a teenager, that's all.

All she cares about is boys and Bacardi Breezers and getting her nails done."

Kate lifted her shoulders. "I cared about more than that, when I was her age."

Mary looked at her with her mouth quirked up at the corner.

"Yes, love," she said. "But you weren't normal."

When Kate closed the door of her flat behind her a few hours later, she stood for a moment, drinking in the peace and serenity of her home. More so than usual, she could feel the calmness that its order inspired in her – the well-being that the neatness, the cleanliness, the carefully-chosen fixtures and ornaments and furniture evoked.

Kate paid for a cleaner to come every week, and she cleaned the place herself, just a quick once-over, every day. It didn't take long. She walked slowly through the small flat, relishing the peace and solitude, the joy of being surrounded by things that she'd chosen with care and attention. She moved about the living room, touching the back of the sofa, the well-filled bookcases, the silver framed photograph of herself on her graduation day from Hendon. She picked it up and regarded it closely, noting her beaming, proud smile, her younger, eager face. *Top of the class, Kate. You couldn't have done that if – if things had been different. You made the right decision – for both of you.*

She went into her small but sparkling bathroom and undressed, dropping her clothes into the wicker laundry basket in the corner. Her jeans and jumper had been clean, but they felt tainted by the hours spent in her mother's house, smelling of smoke and whisky fumes and something else, something indefinable but awful. Kate checked that a clean, white towel hung from the hook by the shower door, ready for her when she stepped out of the cubicle and saw that the clean bathmat was laid on the shining tiles of the floor. She cleaned her teeth and cleaned her face. Before the bathroom mirror clouded over with steam, she regarded her naked body. You couldn't tell. There was nothing on the surface that showed.

For the thousandth time, she pushed away the memories. Shut them away, push them back into the dark. She stepped under the hot gush of water, closing her eyes against the spray. The hot water against her back and neck was so comforting. She watched the foam-laden water stream away from her and down the plughole, and imagined all the mistakes and regrets of the past being carried away with it.

Chapter Eight

GEMMA PHILLIPS LIVED IN A very small townhouse. It was one of a recently-built estate so new that the lawn of the tiny front gardens was like a small, green patchwork quilt, the lines of earth showing between each strip of sod. The houses were what Kate would term "cheaply smart." They looked fresh and desirable because the new paint gleamed, the tiles shone and the windows sparkled. *Give it five years*, thought Kate as she parked the car, *and they'd look considerably less attractive, as the shoddy materials and second-rate design began to show.*

She'd phoned ahead to check that Gemma was at home, for once not at the Fullmans' place. She did at least have a few days off now and then, it seemed. Kate rapped smartly with the new doorknocker, already loose on its nail.

Gemma was slow in answering the door. She peered somewhat suspiciously through the gap between the frame and the door, frowning a little when she saw Kate standing there.

"Good morning," said Kate briskly, stepping forward. This was almost always the easiest way to get in a house quickly – most people didn't have the nerve to hold their ground. Gemma was no exception. She stepped back and Kate pressed on.

"Lovely morning," she said, now fully in the hallway. "I was hoping to have a chat with you about a few things, as I said on the phone. Could we sit down somewhere?"

Obviously accustomed to taking orders, Gemma turned obediently and led her into the small living room. Kate's heels clacked on the laminate flooring. The cheaply smart theme was echoed here in the interior decoration. There was a feature wall of gaudy wallpaper, large silver flowers and red tendrils entwined. There was a glass coffee table, a small black leather sofa and matching armchair. No books, but a pile of glossy magazines in a heap by the armchair. A large flat screen television dominated the small room.

Kate perched herself on the armchair. Gemma sat down hesitantly opposite her. She was wearing black leggings and a fluffy white tunic, belted tightly around her tiny waist. She looked odd in casual wear, not quite comfortable, as if her natural inclination was to be strapped into tight-fitting and uncomfortable suits.

"Do you want tea?" said Gemma, after a moment.

"Yes, lovely, thanks," said Kate. She almost

always agreed to a drink in these circumstances – it gave you a good opportunity to have a look around. As Gemma jumped up and left the room, Kate allowed her gaze to drift about. It snagged on a large cardboard container resting at the side of the sofa, one of the bags which upmarket shops give to their customers to carry their goods away. Kate leaned closer. *Very* upmarket. She noted the Mulberry logo, the satin ribbons that tied the top.

"You've got a new bag?" she asked, as Gemma came back with two steaming mugs of tea.

Gemma nodded, after a moment's hesitation.

"May I see it?" said Kate. "I love Mulberry." A lie, she didn't know a Mulberry from a raspberry, but it might put the girl at her ease.

Gemma hesitated again. Then she pulled out the bag and extracted the handbag from within, all padded sides and gleaming clasps.

"Lovely," said Kate, examining it. "Quite pricey, though, aren't they? Thought you'd treat yourself?"

Gemma nodded. After a moment, she said, "I got my bonus. From Nick."

"Great," said Kate. Then feeling it was time to cut to the chase, she handed the bag back to Gemma and leaned forward.

"I was hoping you could help me, Gemma. In cases like these, it's important that we cover all the angles, so to speak – the background detail, the minutia – you know, in case there's a small point that's really important. Something that otherwise we might miss, but could be vital in solving the case. Do you see what I'm saying?"

Gemma was holding the Mulberry bag on her lap like a shield. She nodded, biting her lip.

Kate went on.

"It's useful to us to get a sort of picture of the people involved, their histories, their habits and so forth. As you've worked for the Fullmans for some years, I thought you'd be able to do this, give me an idea of, well, the sort of people they are. Are you able to do that?"

Gemma was still for a moment. Then, exhaling, she put the bag back into its container and sat back in her chair, crossing her long legs. "Yeah, I can do that," she said. "What did you want to know?"

"Can you tell me about Nick – Mr Fullman? What's his history? Where did he grow up?"

Gemma laughed. "He's an Essex boy. Funny, isn't it? You'd never guess it from the way he speaks. His dad was a builder, but he made money, enough money to send Nick to private school. That's why he talks the way he does, not all – well, Essex, you know. Not all rough."

"So he's from a wealthy family?" Kate asked. "Well, a prosperous family at least."

Gemma nodded. "I guess, although I remember Nick saying his dad lost loads a few years ago, when the credit crunch hit. I think Nick had to lend him some money, bail him out, you know."

"Nick wasn't affected by the property crash?"

"Not so much. He kind of diversified into commercial property then and that didn't seem to take such a hit. He always seemed to have loads of work coming in, anyway."

"You're obviously paid well," said Kate. Gemma looked a little offended, as people tended to do when money was mentioned. "Clearly you also work long hours. You work hard for your money."

Gemma looked mollified. "That's right. It feels like twenty-four seven, this job, sometimes."

"Nick obviously works very hard. Do you think that it ever put a strain on his marriage?"

Gemma sniffed. "Is that what Casey said? She doesn't know, she's born. It's not like she has to work hard. She just gets to sit around and spend his money."

"Do you think Mr Fullman resents that? I mean, does it seem as though he dislikes working so hard?"

Gemma laughed a laugh with no humour in it.

"Nick doesn't resent anything to do with work. He's, like, a workaholic. That's all he thinks about. I'm pretty sure that's why he and his last girlfriend split up, the fact that he spends all his time working. And they'd been together *ages*."

"If that's the case, do you think Mrs Fullman – Casey – finds that difficult?"

"I don't know." Gemma was rolling a strand of hair back and forth between long-nailed fingers. "She doesn't really talk to me much. She doesn't like me."

"Why is that?"

Gemma shrugged. "Probably resents all the time I spend with Nick. We work together a lot, you know. Casey's bound to be a bit jealous. Wives always are."

Kate hesitated, wondering whether to push this further. Ask too probing a question and Gemma would clam up – but then, she needed to know...

"Does Casey have any grounds for jealously?" she asked. "Is there anything more between you and Mr Fullman than perhaps there should be between work colleagues?"

She braced herself for anger and indignation but to her surprise, Gemma seemed quite pleased at the prospect. A small, smug smile showed briefly on her face. After a moment, she shook her head.

"No," she said slowly. "There's nothing like that." She sat up in her chair suddenly. "But just try telling Casey that! She only thinks that because she–" Her voice stopped suddenly, and she dropped her eyes to her lap, picking at the arm of the chair.

Kate raised her eyebrows. "Because she what?" she prompted, after a moment.

"Nothing." Gemma took up her lock of hair again, looking away. "It's nothing."

The gates had clearly clanged shut and that was all she was going to say. Kate paused for a moment, re-running the conversation through her mind. There had been something – what was it? Oh yes...

"You mentioned Nick's ex-girlfriend, Gemma," she said. "You said they'd been together ages. Can you tell me a bit more about her? Presumably you met her."

Gemma's restless fingers stilled for a moment. "Rebecca?" she said. "Yeah, I met her. Several times. She's all right."

"She and Nick were together how long?"

"God, ages. Ten years, maybe?"

"They were married?"

Gemma shook her head. "No, they never got married. Don't know why. I think they were engaged, but they never actually got married." She leant forward a little, conspiratorially. "You know, I'm pretty sure Nick left her for Casey, you know. I don't know for certain, but after they split up, it was only a month or so before Casey appeared on the scene. And it was only a month or so after *that* that she got pregnant."

Kate tapped her fingers on her legs, thinking.

"So it wasn't because of Nick's work that the relationship broke down?"

"I don't know. I'm just guessing. All I know is that Nick was with Rebecca for *years* and then all of a sudden he was with Casey and getting married and having the baby and all that."

Kate nodded.

"How did Rebecca take that?"

Gemma's eyes flickered. "Okay, I guess," she said. She put the end of the lock of hair into her mouth, making her next few words indistinct. "I don't really know. You'll have to ask her."

Kate nodded again. There was a long moment of silence.

"Well, if that's all..." said Gemma, eventually.

Kate leapt to her feet.

"Yes, thank you, Gemma. That's all for now. Thanks for your help."

Was it her imagination or did Gemma relax, just a little? It was probably nothing, but Kate noted it just the same. She pulled on her jacket and gathered up her bag. Gemma stood up as well.

Kate took a last look around the room. A framed photograph on a shelf caught her eye.

"Is that your fiancée?" she asked, gesturing.

Gemma turned around to look. She blushed. "Um, no. That's my brother," she said.

"Oh, right," said Kate. "Nice-looking guy."

Gemma smiled unhappily. "I've got a picture of my fiancée around somewhere if you want to see it," she said after a moment. "His name's Paul."

Kate had already reached the front door.

"Another time, thanks Gemma. Thanks for the tea."

The door shut smartly behind her as she was three steps up the tiny front path. She looked back. Gemma was standing in the living room window, half hidden by the curtains. Kate raised a hand, and the girl turned sharply away, twitching the curtain shut.

Chapter Nine

OLBECK LOOKED UP AT THE sound of Kate's exclamation.

"What's up?"

Kate looked at him, her eyebrows raised. "I've been looking up the prices of Mulberry bags."

Now it was Olbeck's turn to look surprised. "Going to splash out on one, are you?"

"Splash out is right." Kate tapped a few keys to print out the current picture on her computer screen. "If I had a spare few thousand pounds, I'd be spending it on something other than a big leather *bag*, for God's sake. I had no idea they were so expensive."

Olbeck perched himself on the edge of Kate's desk. "Is there a point to this?"

Kate looked up at him, tapping a pencil on the edge of her jaw.

"Gemma Phillips has just bought a new one. A brand new one, of the most expensive type, if I remember correctly."

"And?"

Kate paused. "Well, even with a bonus, would someone on a secretary's wages be able to afford a Mulberry handbag?"

Olbeck shrugged. "She probably stuck it on a credit card." He grinned. "Or maybe she stole it."

"Ha, ha. She had it in the official bag, so I suppose not." Kate pushed her chair back from her desk, sighing. "You're probably right, it's nothing."

Olbeck patted her on the shoulder. "She has an alibi, you know. We checked it out, first thing. She was out on a hot date – we've got witnesses placing her in a restaurant and then clubbing and finally the two of them entering Gemma's house at about four o'clock in the morning from the taxi driver who dropped them off. The whole night accounted for."

Kate half-smiled. "That would be with the fiancée. Paul somebody."

Olbeck snorted. "Fiancée? Hardly. If it's Paul Dinnock you're talking about, and it probably is, it was her first date with the guy. We contacted him and he gave us the full story."

Kate swung round on her chair to stare at him.

"Seriously, it was her first date? With this Paul?"

"Yes. I don't see why he would lie. He was quite open about it, the fact that they'd slept together. I didn't get the impression that it was anything other than a one-night-stand."

"Right," said Kate, slowly.

"Does it matter?" said Olbeck.

"Apart from the fact that she's a liar?"

"Is she?"

"Yes. She told me she was engaged to the guy. She called him her fiancée."

Olbeck raised his eyebrows.

"That's – odd. Slightly odd, at least." A thought seemed to strike him. "Or is it? Don't women lie about that sort of thing all the time?"

Kate grinned. "Well, that's just it. She lied to me about having a fiancée. Is that just embarrassment at being single – I got the impression that that was a bit of a sore subject – or is it that she's just a liar, full stop? And if she is, what else has she lied about?"

She related the particulars of her recent conversation with Gemma to Olbeck. He nodded at various points.

"We need to interview the ex-girlfriend," he said, when Kate had finished speaking. "Don't we?"

"I think so. If only to get a bit more background on the Fullmans. I looked her up, her name's Rebecca D'Arcy-Warner. Minor aristocracy, daughter of a brigadier."

"Let's do it–" Olbeck broke off as the whirlwind that was Anderton was seen and heard approaching down the corridor. "After the meeting."

REBECCA D'ARCY-WARNER HAD AN ATTRACTIVE voice, low and clear and unmistakably upper-class.

For all that, she sounded at first aghast and then suspicious when Kate had explained the reason for her call.

"I hardly think–" Rebecca said and then broke off. "I *heard* about it all, of course. I read about it in the papers. But what on earth has it got to do with *me*?"

Kate attempted to explain. She could almost feel the woman's disbelief radiating down the phone line.

"We're merely trying to gather some more background information," she finished, fearing that her words were falling on stony ground. "As you were with Mr Fullman for so long, you're probably just the person to fill us in on the background details."

"Well," said Rebecca, doubtfully. There was a pause. "I still don't see...but if you think I could help, I don't know–"

"We'd only take up a few minutes of your time, Ms D'Arcy-Warner," said Kate. "Should we come to you?"

"No. I mean, that's not very convenient at the moment. I could come to you – wait, I know. I'll be over at my father's house this afternoon. He lives at Cudston Magna. That's quite near you, isn't it? I could meet you there, if it's really only going to be five minutes. It's just that my father's not well, you see, and I don't want him confused or upset."

Kate hastened to reassure her. She and Olbeck

set off for the hour's drive in his car, only slightly delayed by the now-traditional shovelling of accumulation from the front passenger seat to the back footwells.

Cudston Magna was a tiny village, virtually a hamlet, set amidst rolling green hills and pastures grazed by sheep and cattle. Cudston Manor was a beautiful piece of Georgian architecture with golden stone balustrades and two wings extending out to either side of the original house. Kate got out of the car, feeling insignificant.

Rebecca D'Arcy-Warner looked thoroughly at home here. She came down to meet them, shaking hands with the forthrightness of someone taught social grace from an early age. What surprised Kate was that she was considerably older than Nick Fullman, perhaps by as much as ten years, which meant she must be in her mid to late forties. She was an attractive woman, something of an Amazon in height and build, but with a mane of deep red hair and a broad, high-cheekboned face. She was certainly nothing like Casey Fullman in the looks department.

"I'm sorry for being so abrupt on the phone" she said, ushering them through the front door. "It just didn't seem like anything I could assist you with and I was worried about my father being worried, if you see what I mean. He's quite elderly, and I don't like him to be upset in any way. It's not good for him."

Kate nodded. Rebecca led them into a small, charming sitting room.

"I'm not sure how I can help you," she said, sitting down and clasping her hands together. There were no rings on her fingers. Kate remembered that she'd never actually been married to Nick Fullman.

Kate began.

"We were hoping you could tell us something about Nick Fullman. We'd like to know more of his background, from people who knew him well. I believe you were with him for some considerable time?"

Rebecca nodded. "Eleven years." Her face flickered for a moment and then cleared. "We met just before the millennium. We both belonged to a property investor's network –that's where we met."

"You and Mr Fullman were engaged?" said Olbeck.

"Yes. We were engaged for two years."

"But – forgive me – you never married?"

Rebecca shook her head. She was sitting very upright and very still, her hands gripping one another. "No, we never actually got married."

"Why was that?"

She blinked. "Is that relevant?"

"I'm sorry but it may be."

Rebecca looked away. "I hardly see how." There was a pause and then she said, "Well, it's old news now, anyway. I'm not sure why it didn't work out.

We just drifted apart really. It wasn't anything very dramatic."

"You didn't have any children together?"

Kate was watching closely. As she asked the question she saw the minute jerk of Rebecca's shoulders, almost too small to notice. Then the movement was gone, and Rebecca answered the question in a calm, steady tone.

"No, no children." She laughed, rather harshly. "I'm not very maternal, I'm afraid. Children have never really been in my life plan."

Olbeck nodded. "So there were no hard feelings between you and Mr Fullman when your relationship ended?"

"Well, nothing out of the ordinary. I mean, it was *painful*. We'd been together for years. It took me a while to recover. I mean, when your life's being going one way and then all of a sudden, there's an enormous detour...that takes a while to get over, doesn't it?" She gazed at them both, earnestly. Her words rang with sincerity. "But after the dust had settled, I could see – we could both see – that it was really for the best."

Kate waited for a moment and then asked, "Did you resent Mr Fullman marrying so soon after your relationship broke up?"

Rebecca blinked again. "Of course not." She gave a rather stagy laugh. "I mean – well, I wouldn't want to be uncharitable, but it did seem rather *too* sudden. And then of course, the baby was born so perhaps they had to get married, although in this day and age it doesn't seem very likely, does it? That she trapped him into it, I mean." Her gaze fell to her clasped hands. "No doubt he knew what he was doing."

"Are you still in regular contact with Mr Fullman?"

Rebecca laughed again. She seemed to use laughter as punctuation rather than as a method of expressing joy or excitement.

"I'm afraid I haven't seen Nick since we split up. Not since he moved out and that was, oh, nearly two years ago now."

Kate cleared her throat. "I understand that Mr Fullman is something of a, shall we say, a workaholic? He works incredibly hard?"

Rebecca nodded. "He works very hard. Such long hours...that was always a bit of a sore point between us. I mean, I have my business – I'm a property investor – and that takes up a fair bit of time but I have a *life* as well, you know. Nick doesn't ever stop. That's why he's so successful, of course. He's driven." Her voice faltered for a moment. "He works out what he wants and then he goes and gets it. That's admirable, in a way. It's something I learnt from him, that if you really want something, you have to put your all into it. You have to go out and get it. No matter what it takes."

The door to the sitting room opened with a creak, making them all look over towards it. An elderly man paused with his hand on the door handle, peering at them.

"Rebecca?" he said, in a gentle voice, quavering a little. Rebecca jumped up.

"It's fine, Dad. These are the people I was telling you about."

The man, clearly Brigadier D'Arcy-Warner, stood for a moment, his head swinging a little from side to side. Although in his eighties, or perhaps even older, he still had a head of copious black hair, scarcely greyed at the temples. Rebecca turned to the police officers.

"Well, if that was all, perhaps we could call it a day?"

Her voice was anxious. Kate and Olbeck exchanged glances and got up.

"Who are these people?" said Brigadier D'Arcy-Warner. He didn't say it in a rude fashion, but Rebecca blushed, the pink of her cheeks clashing with the red of her hair.

"It doesn't matter, Daddy, they're leaving now. Go back to the sitting room and I'll bring you through a cup of tea. Go on now." He hesitated, one faintly shaking hand resting on the door handle. "I'll bring you through a cup of tea."

The Brigadier nodded vaguely and turned away,

out of sight. They all heard his hesitant footsteps fade from hearing.

Rebecca remained standing.

"He has dementia," she said, to their unspoken question. "Not too severe as yet, but he gets very confused...very confused. I try and keep him in a routine, calm and ordered, you know. It helps."

"Does he live here alone?" asked Olbeck.

"No, he has a home help and carers that come in every day. And of course, I'm here most of the time. I can set my own hours, so I'm here pretty much every day."

"You don't live here?"

"No, I have my own place just outside of Tornford." She half-smiled. "Nick and I bought it together, actually. But he moved out, obviously, when we split up and he bought that modern monstrosity."

Kate pricked up her ears.

"You've been to Mr Fullman's house, then?"

Rebecca shrugged. "Just the once. I had to drop off some of his things." She grimaced. "Once was enough."

Olbeck nodded. "It's routine," he said. "But I have to ask you where you were on the night of the crime. Saturday, the fourteenth of January."

Kate expected another outburst of incredulity but Rebecca just sighed. "Yes, I thought you might ask me that," she said. "I can see that you have to

– what's the phrase? Eliminate people from your enquiries." Olbeck nodded encouragingly. Rebecca sighed again. "I'm afraid that, as usual, I was here, with my father. I stayed the night. I usually do if I get here late."

"Is there anyone who can verify your presence here?"

"I'm afraid not." She sounded regretful.

"What about your father?"

Rebecca looked shocked.

"Well, yes. He could confirm it – for what it's worth. But as I've said, he has dementia. And, if it's not essential, I'd really prefer that you didn't ask him. It would confuse him and if he knew anything about the – well, the murder – it would upset him terribly."

What isn't essential in a murder case? Kate thought. She and Olbeck left it at that, shaking hands and handing over their cards as a matter of routine. Rebecca watched them drive away from the front door, holding her arms across her body, one elbow in each hand.

"What did you think?" asked Kate, as they drove onto the main road.

Olbeck shrugged. "Hard-nosed career type, if you ask me." He looked over at her and grinned. "Like you."

Kate half laughed to cover her sudden intake of breath. Was that the image she gave out? *Why not, Kate*, she asked herself. *Isn't that what it's all about? Isn't that what you wanted?*

"She's got no alibi," was all she said.

"We could ask the Major."

"Brigadier. But I agree with her that it's probably not worth our while."

Olbeck flicked on the indicator. "I got the impression that it was a pretty lukewarm sort of relationship. Her and Fullman, I mean. What motive would she have for kidnapping his kid and killing his nanny?"

It was Kate's turn to shrug. "You're right. Still, that's one more off the list."

"Onwards and upwards."

They drove in silence for a moment.

"I get the impression you don't really care for ambitious women," said Kate, after a long moment of thought. Was it too soon to be having this kind of conversation? The last thing she wanted to be was antagonistic.

Olbeck looked astonished. "Where did you get that impression?" he said.

Kate spread her hands. "I don't know. Just what you said back there – and you having what sounds like a nice little domestic goddess at home." She glanced at him sideways. "Am I wrong?"

Olbeck spluttered. "You could not be *more* wrong. God, you make me sound like a complete sexist."

"Sorry."

They drove in silence for another minute.

"God," said Olbeck, shaking his head. "I am so not like that. Kate, you really couldn't be more wrong. I'm all for the emancipated woman, believe me."

Kate laughed, relieved at his tone. "Sorry. I misread you."

"S'alright."

The car turned, slowing. Kate drummed her fingers on her knees.

"So, what does Jo do?" she asked just for something to say.

Olbeck looked over at her. "Acting," he said, briefly.

"Really? God, that's interesting. Would she have been in anything I've seen?" Kate reflected for a moment. "Actually, probably not. I don't watch much TV, and I can't remember when I last went to the cinema. Or theatre."

They'd arrived at the station and Olbeck swung the car into a parking space.

"Come on," he said, clearly ready to move on from the subject. "Paperwork time."

"Oh, joy."

Chapter Ten

KATE WAS HALFWAY THROUGH HER reports when her phone rang. She placed the voice on the end of the line immediately.

"What can I do for you, Ms Darcy-Warner?"

"Call me Rebecca, please. I'm sorry to bother you but I–" She hesitated for a moment. Kate sat up a little, reaching for her pen.

Rebecca continued. "I'm afraid I wasn't entirely truthful earlier. No, that's not correct, I didn't lie. I'm afraid I didn't tell you a few things. That's probably lying by omission, isn't it?"

"Never mind about that now, Rebecca. Can you tell me now?"

"It's probably not even relevant..."

"Let me be the judge of that. Please tell me and then you'll have done your duty." Kate said that last with a smile in her voice, trying to break down the other woman's reserve.

"Yes," said Rebecca, hesitating again. Then she plunged on. "It's just that – Nick – well, there was another reason we split up. There always is, isn't there?"

"Yes, indeed. And that other reason was?"

"Well– basically, he was keeping some very odd company. Some very reprehensible company. I didn't approve."

"Can you be more specific?"

"He said they were business associates but – I just didn't like them. I work in the property business too and you hear things...these men were notorious." Rebecca lowered her voice so that Kate had to strain to hear her. "They were gangsters."

"Gangsters?"

"Oh it sounds so melodramatic, doesn't it? But they were definitely not the people to get on the wrong side of."

"And Mr Fullman was working with them?"

"Well, I don't know about working with them – but he was definitely meeting them. He met them several times. They even came to our house once before I put my foot down."

"Can you give me their names?"

"I'm afraid not, not definitely. You see, I refused to listen when Nick tried to talk about them. I really didn't approve. I think they were called Costa, or Costas. Something like that."

Kate tried to push for a few more details but Rebecca insisted she didn't know any more. Eventually Kate gave up and thanked her for calling.

CELINA GRACE

"You're welcome," said Rebecca. There was a slight pause and Kate was just about to say goodbye before Rebecca said suddenly, "It's funny, about Nick. He looks so, so adult and successful and together. You wouldn't have thought anyone could put anything over on him. But underneath it all, he's just a scared little boy."

Kate's eyebrows went up. "Is that–" she began, but Rebecca was speaking again.

"Just a scared, uncertain little boy. Perhaps that's why he needed so much *mothering*." For a moment, bitterness pervaded her voice. "Anyway, I hope I've been of help."

Kate assured her that she had, and they said goodbye. Kate stared at the replaced handset for a moment, tapping her pen on the edge of the desk and thinking. Then she lifted the telephone again and asked to speak to Anderton.

"COSTA?"

"That's right, sir. She said 'Costa' or 'Costas.'"

Anderton and Olbeck exchanged glances. Kate interpreted it.

"You know the name then?"

"Yes," said Anderton. "You're new here, DS Redman, so I'll forgive you for not picking this up. " He smiled briefly. "The Costa brothers are known to us."

"What have they done?"

Anderton looked at Olbeck, who took up the conversation.

"Fraud, arson, extortion – or at least, that's what we've tried to charge them with at various times. Sometimes successfully and sometimes not. They're extremely wealthy and have a crack team of lawyers on their side."

"They've both spent time in prison," said Anderton. "Both are currently free, though. And they were free on the night of January 14th."

"Hmm," said Kate.

"Hmm, is right," said Anderton. "A lead worth following up, I think. Talk to Nick Fullman about his association with the Costa. Ask him why he didn't think this little nugget of information was worth mentioning when we questioned him before."

"Would you suspect them of something like this, sir?"

Anderton shrugged. "I don't believe they've ever stooped to murder or kidnapping *before*. That's not to say it's out of the question. It's a lead."

Kate and Olbeck nodded and went to get up.

"Wait," said Anderton. "While you're with Mr Fullman, you can ask him about this little matter as well." He reached into a desk drawer and withdrew a small sheet of white paper, enclosed in an evidence bag. He handed it to Olbeck, who smoothed it out on the desk top and read it aloud.

119

"'*Ask Fullman about Councillor Jones*'. What's this? When did you receive this, sir?"

"This morning, in an anonymous envelope, in the post. Addressed to me."

"Councillor Jones?" said Kate. "That's the–" She groped for a moment. "That's the guy he was having a drink with on the night of Charlie's disappearance, right?"

Anderton nodded.

"Councillor Gary Jones is a District Councillor for Abbeyford. He's on the planning committee and the brownfield regeneration committee. Nick Fullman works in property. Now, there may be nothing more natural than the two of them being buddies, but I want it looked into. If someone wants to cause trouble, enough to go to the effort of writing, or typing, an anonymous note, there may be something in it."

He tweaked the note from under Olbeck's fingers and waved a hand at them both. "Off you go, then."

Outside Anderton's office, Kate turned to Olbeck.

"Phew," she said. "Where to start?"

Olbeck began to count on his fingers.

"We've got Casey to question about Ali Saheed, Fullman to question about the Costa brothers and Councillor Jones, Mrs Bright to question full-stop, Councillor Jones to question about Nick Fullman and the Costa brothers to question if only for a reason for their revolting existence."

Kate rubbed her forehead.

"Where do you want to start?"

Olbeck started to walk down the corridor. Kate hurried after him.

"I'll take the Costa brothers." He shuddered. "God, for my sins. Theo or Jerry can do Councillor Jones. Why don't you do Casey and Mrs Bright and we'll track down Nick Fullman together?"

"Fine," said Kate. "Let's check back later."

She said goodbye and hurried off to find her car keys.

Chapter Eleven

THE PAPARAZZI AT THE GATES of the Fullmans' house had thinned in numbers slightly, and their replacement was, at first sight, more picturesque. A heap of blooms, a mountain of flowers: bouquets, baskets, single-stemmed white roses. Blue ribbons everywhere, tied to the trees and the fence and the gateposts.

As Kate drove through, she caught sight of a tiny blue teddy bear with white, fluffy paws. A middle-aged couple stood by the makeshift shrine, reading the inscriptions on the bouquets. Who were they mourning, these people who'd brought the flowers? Dita or Charlie? *He's not dead*, said Kate to herself, fiercely, because at the thought of Charlie dead, something seemed to collapse inside of her. She knew, logically, that he probably was. But logic didn't seem to have anything to do with it. *I can't think of him dead*, she thought, fingers clenched on the steering wheel. *I can't.*

She thought of all the blue ribbons fluttering

in the cold January wind and felt something else, a surge of anger. What good were ribbons? What possible difference would tying a ribbon around a tree make? Would it get them one step closer to Charlie? *Stupid, stupid*, she hissed through gritted teeth, parking the car a little too abruptly by the front door.

The sight of Casey shocked her out of her anger. *Zombie* was the word that first came to mind when the door opened. Hollowed eyes, blonde hair darkened and flattened by grease, Casey swayed a little on her feet. She turned, saying nothing, and walked back through the house like a somnambulist, the dirty ends of her tracksuit trousers trailing on the floor.

Mrs Bright was there in the kitchen, perched on a stool by the breakfast bar, the local paper spread out before her and a half empty glass of orange juice in front of her. Kate greeted her and asked where Mr Fullman was.

Mrs Bright rolled her eyes. "At work? Where else is he ever?"

Kate nodded. She hesitated again, wondering whether to question Mrs Bright or to follow Casey. She decided on the latter. Casey worried her, seriously worried her.

She knocked on the door of the bedroom, although it was half open and she could see the dirty soles of Casey's feet dangling off the edge of the enormous bed. There was no answer so she pushed open the door.

Casey was lying face down, her head buried in the pillows. Kate said her name, gently at first and then with more urgency. At last, Casey turned her head to look at her.

"What?"

"Casey, please sit up. I need to speak to you."

In the end, she had to help her up, almost prop her against the headboard. Casey's pupils were huge and she stared blearily ahead, saying nothing. Kate was uncomfortably reminded of a doll from her childhood, a rare toy she'd been given by a neighbour, which had had the same blank stare, the same empty eyes.

"Casey," she said once more. "I told you we'd find Charlie for you and we will. But you have to help us. I need to talk to you about Ali Saheed."

That broke Casey's stupor. She flicked a frightened sideways glance at Kate.

"Why?"

"It's important."

"I told you, he couldn't have done this. He wouldn't."

"Why would you say that?"

Casey paused for a second.

"He always said family was important, even though he didn't have any kids of his own. He likes children. He was really happy for me when I got pregnant. He said so."

Kate sighed inwardly.

"People don't always mean what they say, Casey. Believe me, as a police officer I know that."

Casey started to cry.

"This is a nightmare, it's a nightmare. I can't believe it's happening. I think I'm going mad."

Kate fought against the urge to hug her, pat her on the back, rock her into comfort again.

"I just need to know if–"

Casey interrupted her, her words barely audible over loud sobs.

"I'm being punished. This is my punishment."

Kate frowned. "What do you mean by that, Casey?"

Casey shook her head, crying louder.

"Is it something that you feel you've done?" Kate hesitated, unsure of whether to go any further. Should she call Olbeck or Anderton? Was this going to be a confession? She could feel her heart rate begin to speed up, the sickness rising in her stomach. What to do?

She pressed on.

"Is it something you've done to – to Charlie?"

Casey shook her head again, almost screaming

"No, no! I would never hurt my baby, never. What are you, *sick*?"

She rolled away from Kate, burying her head in

the pillows again. She said something else but it was too muffled for Kate to make out.

Kate sat back, thinking hard. Guilt, but not at something to do with the baby...if she was telling the truth. She ran through the possibilities, internally. What the hell, she was probably right...

She pulled at Casey's arm, speaking sharply. "Casey. Casey! Sit up, please. I need to ask you something."

After a few moments, Casey sat up again. She looked at Kate, sullenly.

Kate took the bull by the horns. "Did you have an affair with Ali Saheed?"

The expression on Casey's face, aghast and guilty, told her everything she needed to know. After a moment, Casey dropped her eyes. She gave a tiny nod of the head, so tiny it was almost imperceptible.

Kate sighed. "When was this?"

Casey looked up at her for a split second and then looked away.

"Not since the baby," she said quickly.

"Not since the birth or not since the pregnancy?"

Casey's voice wobbled. "Not since the birth. Of course not. Not for months."

"Was it just a one-off?"

"No. We – we were together on and off for years. But secretly, you know. I don't know why..." Her voice faded for a second. "I don't know why we didn't get together properly. Ali said it wouldn't be very professional."

But shagging his clients was? Kate mentally filed away her sarcastic comment without voicing it.

"So you've been in an on-going relationship with Mr Saheed for years?" A nod from Casey. "Does Mr Fullman know?"

Casey blanched. "God, no. He would kill me." She grabbed at Kate's arm, her eyes huge. "You won't tell him, will you? Please God, don't tell him. He'd kill me." She started to hyperventilate. "Oh Christ, oh God, why did I tell you? Don't tell him, please don't tell him..."

Kate hastened to soothe her as best she could.

"Casey, please don't worry. We'll do all we can to keep this between us."

Casey put her head in her hands. The part of her hair showed a inch-thick strip of dark brown hair, visible against the blonde streaks.

"I can't believe this," she whispered. "I know my affair was wrong but I *know* Ali, I know he wouldn't do this."

Kate took a deep breath. "I need to know all about this, Casey. Can you tell me?"

Silence from the woman on the bed.

"Casey. You have to talk to me. When did you two first, er, get together?"

Casey kept her head in her hands, but she began to speak, slowly and with a gasp in her voice.

"It was about five years ago now. I needed an agent and someone told me about him and so I rang him up. And then we met and there was, oh, I dunno, an instant attraction, I guess. And he was a good agent. He got me lots of work. Magazines and that TV show. We were never really a couple though, you know. We were just, just..."

Kate groped for the appropriate term. "Friends with benefits?"

Casey nodded. "Sort of. I mean, I guess I knew he had other girlfriends and I used to date a few guys myself. But somehow we always ended up sleeping together again. And then I met Nick and got pregnant, and then it just seemed wrong. I just couldn't do it any more."

"So you sacked him as your agent?"

Casey nodded. "I thought that would be the easiest way for both of us."

Mentally, Kate rolled her eyes. "You didn't really expect Mr Saheed to think that? He loses his client and his girlfriend in one go?"

Casey put her hands up to her eyes again. "I don't know," she cried. "I just had to, I couldn't – couldn't have Nick finding out, you don't know what he would have done."

Kate's antenna went up, quivering.

"You think Mr Fullman would have reacted angrily?" *Stupid question, Kate.* She rephrased it. "I mean, obviously he would be angry, very angry, but you were scared of his reaction?" Casey didn't react. "Physically scared?"

Casey did nothing for a moment. Then she gave another small nod.

Kate drummed her fingers on her knees.

"Does Mr Fullman ever threaten you? Is he ever violent towards you? Or abusive in any way?"

Casey took her hands down from her face, wiping the tears from under her eyes.

"No," she sniffed. "He's not that bad."

Kate opened her mouth to ask another question but a knock on the door made them both jump. Mrs Bright stood in the doorway.

"Just came to see if you wanted a cup of tea?" she said, her eyes going straight to Casey's tear-stained face.

"We're fine, thank you, Mrs Bright," said Kate, inwardly cursing her for the interruption. The moment had gone, she could feel it.

"I want one," said Casey loudly, confirming Kate's realisation that the moment of confession was over. She got up from the bed, allowing Casey to swing her legs to the floor and followed her through to the kitchen.

Mrs Bright made Casey a cup of tea, and her daughter took it wordlessly. The brief spasm of defiance that she'd displayed seemed to have dissipated. She eyed Kate for a moment, blankly, and then turned and trailed away, back to the bedroom.

Kate let her go. She had Mrs Bright to talk to and this would be the perfect opportunity.

"I will have a cup, if there's one going, Mrs Bright," she said.

Sheila Bright nodded. Kate watched her make the tea. There was a huge, domed cluster of diamonds on her ring finger, sparkling over the other gold and platinum rings that cluttered her fingers.

"Are you married, Mrs Bright?" asked Kate.

Sheila handed her a mug of tea, the bag still in it, liquid slopping over the side.

"I was," she said, briefly. "Got divorced years ago."

"Is Casey your only child?"

A nod.

"So Charlie is your only grandchild?"

The artificially smooth face contracted for a moment. "Yes."

"It must be very distressing for you," said Kate. She took a sip of the awful tea. "We're doing all we can to find him."

Mrs Bright nodded. Kate pressed on.

"How did Casey find motherhood?" She revised her question quickly. "How is Casey finding motherhood? It's quite hard, the first time, isn't it?"

"She's okay," said Mrs Bright, non-committally.

"As all right as she can be. She has a lot of help. Had a lot, poor Dita."

"Does Mr Fullman help her out with the baby?"

Mrs Bright laughed soundlessly. It was the first sign of animation she'd shown.

"Nick, help out? When would he have time? He's always at work isn't he? Besides..." She stopped talking, raising one glittering finger to her mouth for a moment.

"Besides, Mrs Bright?" prompted Kate.

Sheila Bright flicked her a sideways glance. "It's difficult for men, isn't it?" she said, evasively. "They don't always deal with babies too well. You know."

"I'm afraid I don't know, Mrs Bright. Can you elaborate?"

"Well, they get jealous, don't they? Only natural if they've been the centre of attention for so long. All of a sudden, there's someone else getting all the attention, isn't there? It's no wonder some men feel a bit pushed out."

"You're saying Mr Fullman felt pushed out when Charlie was born?"

Sheila Bright's face clearly wasn't capable of showing extreme emotion, but she looked a little uneasy. "Well, sort of," she said. "Nothing bad or anything. I had the same thing with my ex-husband when Casey was born. It's normal."

"Is it?"

"Yes, it is," said Sheila Bright, shortly.

Kate put her mug down. "Do you think Mr Fullman resented his baby?"

"Don't be stupid," said Sheila Bright. Then she coloured a little. "Sorry. I didn't mean anything. All I meant was that men find it hard, don't they, that's all. Nothing worse than that. They get over it, anyway, once the baby's been here for a while. It all settles down."

They get over it, anyway... Kate thought about that as she drove away from the house. Did they? Had Nick Fullman gotten over it? Had he even had a chance? Was the bit about his behaviour true and, if it was, did it mean anything? She turned the car lights on, illuminating the road ahead, and pulled out of the driveway, keeping her face turned from the gates and the fluttering mass of ribbons, staring straight ahead into the gathering dusk.

Chapter Twelve

"INTERESTING," SAID ANDERTON. KATE AND Olbeck were sat in his office, ostensibly facing his desk but actually turning this way and that in their chairs to keep him in view as he paced up and down.

"I don't know why I didn't think of it earlier," said Olbeck. "Saheed was obviously pretty cut up about the fact that he never saw Casey Fullman anymore."

A search of Ali Saheed's flat had yielded nothing of interest, except a half-full wrap of cocaine and some fairly vanilla pornography. Kate swivelled in her seat, trying to catch Anderton's eye.

"Casey is clearly scared of her husband," she said. "She said several times 'He'll kill me.' It wouldn't surprise me if he's abusive, emotionally abusive if not physically."

"And where is your evidence for that, DS Redman? A lot of wives would be very scared of their husbands finding out they'd had a five-year affair. It doesn't mean that they're all married to perpetrators of domestic violence."

Kate took a deep breath. "No, I appreciate that, but–"

"But what? You have no evidence of abuse. None. Dig around if you must, talk to a few more people. You can't assume from a throwaway comment – a throwaway comment from an extremely emotionally distraught woman – that it means anything of significance."

"Actually, sir," said Olbeck, seeing that Kate was momentarily wrong-footed. "It would be useful to get a bit more background on this development. Casey says no one knew, but in my experience, someone always knows."

Kate was thinking hard. There was something Gemma Phillips had said – what was it? She scrolled back through her mental files, searching for the pertinent phrase. What was it? She thought of her last interview with Gemma: the Mulberry bag, the false fiancée, the smile at the suggestion of an affair with Nick – *ah*. That was it. What had Gemma said when confronted with that very suggestion? She'd retorted something about it being Casey who'd told Kate that. What else? *But just try telling Casey that! She only thinks that because she–*

"Gemma Phillips," she said, slowly. "She knows. Or she knows something. I have a feeling she knows more about this than she's letting on. I'll talk to her again."

Anderton finally came to a halt and looked at her.

"Do that," he said, briefly. "Where are we with the other things?"

Olbeck consulted his notes.

"Jerry interviewed Gary Jones about his association with Nick Fullman. Insisted there was nothing more than a business acquaintanceship and that he wanted Nick's advice on investing in property. They were apparently discussing buy to let investments during their meeting on January 14th. Nothing else. "

"Have you spoken to Fullman about this, yet?"

"Not yet, sir."

"Well, do it. Quickly. What about the Costa brothers?"

"My report's here, sir." He handed over a file. Kate flashed him a glance, and he shook his head, minutely.

"Fine," said Anderton. "Redman, what about Gemma Phillips?"

"I haven't had a chance yet, sir. I was with Casey and Mrs Bright yesterday. I'm going there right now."

"Right," said Anderton, glancing through Olbeck's file. He didn't look up at her. "Get on with it, then."

KATE RANG THE FULLMANS' HOUSE and got Mrs Bright on the end of the line.

"Gemma?" said Mrs Bright in answer to Kate's question. "No, she's not here today. I don't know if she's been in today or not, to be honest."

Kate asked, fairly hopelessly, to speak to Nick, and to her surprise was speaking with him in a matter of seconds.

"Nick Fullman here."

What are you doing at home? She managed not to voice the question with some difficulty. Instead, she asked whether Gemma was expected in the office at all today.

"She's not been in today," said Nick, conventionally enough. Then his tone began to change to one of outrage. "She's been really slack as a matter of fact, asked me for a couple of days holiday, which I could really have done without at this time, but I said yeah, no problem. Then she's supposed to be back today and she doesn't turn up, she's not answering her phone..."

"She hasn't been in contact?" said Kate. She was conscious of a faint, creeping unease.

Nick Fullman's hard, angry tones came down the line.

"Not a phone call, not a text or an email. I'd go round to her place myself but I can't leave Casey. I don't know what's the matter with her, She's not like this usually."

"I'll call on Ms Phillips myself," said Kate. Two memories popped up: Casey's white face as she said *Don't tell him, he'll kill me* and Gemma's face at the window of her house, looking furtively out at Kate from behind the curtains. That creeping feeling of unease was getting stronger.

"What's up?" said Olbeck, as she put the phone down. Kate explained in a few sentences and he nodded his head.

"Think we ought to take a look?"

Kate was already gathering up her coat. "I do. Let's go."

They didn't talk much on the drive there. The house looked as normal when they parked outside, a light on in the front room, the closed curtains glowing gently. Kate and Olbeck looked at each other.

"Come on," said Kate, and they got out of the car and knocked at the door.

There was no answer.

Kate banged the cheap, loose brass knocker once more. Then once more. Then she knelt and shouted through the letterbox.

"Gemma! It's DS Redman, Kate Redman. Are you there?"

Silence. Olbeck moved to the living room window and knelt, peering through the minute gap between the edge of the curtain and the windowsill. Then he straightened up.

"Let's get that door open," he said, and something in his voice made Kate shudder involuntarily.

The two of them got the door open in three shoulder charges. Inside the house was warm and stuffy, a faint breath of something in the air almost too intangible to notice. There was still enough for the two of them to approach the half-open living room door with dread.

Gemma Phillips lay slackly on the sofa, one outflung arm brushing the floor. Pulled tightly around her throat was a silk scarf, its marbled blue and green pattern horribly matched to the cyanotic hue of her dead face. Her mouth hung open and her eyes were closed.

Kate and Olbeck stood and looked for a long moment. Kate could hear her own fast breathing echoed in Olbeck's but neither of them said anything – they just stood and looked at poor Gemma, lying there dead on the sofa until the silence stretched out interminably and Olbeck finally reached for his phone.

Chapter Thirteen

"SHE WAS KILLED WITH THIS," said Doctor Telling, indicating the silk scarf coiled incongruously in a metal kidney bowl on the autopsy table. "Obviously. But it wouldn't surprise me if she was drugged first. I'll have to wait until the stomach contents have been analysed before I can say for certain. But from the posture, the looseness of the limbs...yes, I'd say it was highly possible she was drugged first."

Anderton nodded. They were all there in the autopsy theatre – Kate, Olbeck and Anderton – watching Doctor Telling perform her work on Gemma Phillips.

"So she wouldn't have known anything about it?" said Kate. She looked at Gemma's face, plainer than ever now stripped of life and make-up, and felt a terrible sadness.

Doctor Telling shrugged her thin shoulders.

"I'm not sure. I wouldn't have thought so."

"I hope you're right," muttered Kate, almost under her breath. Olbeck patted her on the shoulder.

"Poor girl," he said. Kate thought he was referring to Gemma, but who knew?

Back in the station control room, Anderton regarded the scene of crime photographs from Gemma's house.

"No sign of a struggle," he said. "No sign of forced entry. She almost certainly knew her killer."

"Almost certainly?" said Kate. "I wouldn't have thought there was any doubt about it."

Anderton glanced at her.

"No doubt you are right, DS Redman. I never like to make emphatic statements such as yours until I'm absolutely certain of the facts."

"That's right," said Olbeck, and Kate gave him an annoyed glance. "We're assuming that Gemma's murder is a direct result of Dita's murder and Charlie's kidnapping. But what if it's not? What it it's completely unrelated, just a bad coincidence? What if one of her internet dating buddies killed her?"

"Oh, come *on,*" said Kate. "That's ridiculous. It's got to be connected."

"We have to look at every possibility."

"Mark's right," said Anderton, interrupting Kate as she was taking a deep breath, about to launch into a tirade. "But you're right as well. I want you to have a look at her bank statements. Go through them with a fine-tooth comb if necessary. Go through her *house* with a fine-tooth comb. Get the evidence."

Kate shook herself, trying to calm down. "Yes, sir."

"Get on with it then. I'll swear the warrant for you."

Kate remained standing. "What about the Fullmans?"

Anderton glanced at her.

"I'll deal with them. Get on with looking in Gemma's affairs. Olbeck, you too."

"Has Nick Fullman got an alibi for the night of Gemma's murder?" asked Kate, stubbornly.

"Are you trying to tell me how to do my job, DC Redman?"

"No, sir." *Stop it Kate, you're antagonising him. Just leave it.* "I'm just anxious to cover all bases, like you said." *Just shut up.*

"Come on," said Olbeck, propelling her towards the door. "Bank first. You can drive."

Out in the corridor, he shook his head. "God, girl, don't you know when to shut up?"

Kate twitched her shoulders crossly. "Oh, leave it out, will you? It's just – you know we need to look at the Fullmans. At Nick Fullman particularly."

Olbeck raised his eyebrows.

"But not Casey?"

Kate shook her head.

"Well," said Olbeck. "You're probably right.

But you can't go steaming in and accusing people without evidence, as well you know."

"Are you telling me I don't know that?" said Kate. "For fuck's sake, Mark. That's why we need to be checking alibis and so forth."

Olbeck chuckled. "That's the first time I've heard you swear."

"I can assure you that it won't be the last."

"Look, Anderton's no fool. He'll dig up anything that necessary."

They had reached the car. Kate flung herself into the driver's seat.

"You suspect him, then?" said Olbeck quietly as he got in next to her.

Kate glanced over. "Don't you?"

"It's possible," said Olbeck cautiously.

Kate made a noise indicative of impatience but said nothing else, putting her foot down on the accelerator.

The manager at Gemma's bank was forthcoming and led them to a private room at the back of the bank with the paperwork all ready for them. Kate spread the statements out on the table and waited for the manager to leave.

"Plain as day," she said as the door shut. She pointed. "Look, here and here. Large cash sums deposited."

"Blackmail payments," said Olbeck.

Kate nodded. "It's possible. As you might say."

He gave her a half-grin.

"The dates tally. Look, the first thousand goes in here, two days after Dita's death. Then another a week later. Big one, that one. She must have used some of the cash to buy that Mulberry bag."

"Someone didn't want to pay out any more and killed her instead?"

"It looks like it. She must have known who took Charlie, or killed Dita, or both." Kate stared across the room at the bank wall, unseeingly. "I *knew* she knew something. Secretaries always know something. I should have pushed her harder to talk."

"You didn't know she was going to be killed. Everyone's always hiding something in a murder case, you know that. It's finding out what's important and what's not that's difficult."

"I know. It's just..." she let the sentence tail off in a sigh.

Olbeck gathered up the papers.

"I know. It's shit. But let's get this stuff back to the station and get to her house."

"It has to be someone in that house," said Kate as they left the building.

Olbeck looked across at her.

"You're probably right," he said. "But we need to-"

"Get the evidence, I know," said Kate. They

143

got into the car. "What happened with the Costa brothers?"

Olbeck exhaled loudly. "The usual. Superficial charm, then outrage and bombast at the accusation that they had anything to do with this case at all. 'I've got two sons of my own, Detective Sergeant Olbeck', as if that precluded any parent from doing anything criminal at all at any time. Both with rock-solid alibis for the night of the 14th."

"What about the night Gemma was killed?"

"How would I know? It hadn't happened when I interviewed them."

Kate slapped her forehead. "Duh. Sorry."

"You buffoon."

Kate grinned, despite herself. "You've got a good vocabulary for a copper."

"Oh, cheers," he said sarcastically. "'For a copper'. Do you mind? I get enough of that at home."

Gemma's little house had a forlorn appearance, made worse by the police tape cordon and the little straggle of curious onlookers. Kate wondered whether people would come and tie ribbons to the railings outside to join the few pathetic bunches of flowers that had been laid on the pavement. Pink ones, naturally. She gritted her teeth.

Ravinder Cheetam, Rav to his colleagues, and Jerry Hindley were already there, working methodically through cupboards and drawers. They nodded at Kate and Olbeck.

"There's more designer stuff here than you shake a stick at," said Rav. He held up a Prada bag. "Clothes in the bedroom. New iPad. Looks like she was spending for England."

Kate stirred the tissue paper that had drifted onto the floor with her foot. "Shame she never got to enjoy any of it."

"Right."

"Jane and Theo are interviewing the neighbours," said Jerry, to Olbeck. Kate couldn't put her finger on it, but she had the impression that Jerry didn't much like her. It annoyed her, but this wasn't the time or place to worry about it.

"I'll look upstairs," she said.

Gemma's bedroom was mostly white and pink, the bed unmade, a hot-pink quilted throw half-slipped to the floor. A grubby pair of slippers with the backs trodden down peeked out from under the bed. The sight of them made Kate feel sad again. She began to work through the bedside cupboard, finding the usual stash: condoms, tissues, old pens, broken necklaces, a vibrator shoved right to the back. In the base of the cupboard were several self-help books dealing with relationships. More glossy magazines. An older model mobile phone.

She moved to the wardrobe, which was stuffed with clothes, mostly the formal work suits that

Gemma had so often been seen in, but some dresses, shirts, short skirts to show off those long legs. What seemed like hundreds of pairs of shoes. Kate thought of her own pathetic collection of footwear at home, a black pair of heels, work shoes, trainers, Birkenstocks. Sometimes she felt as if she was slightly weird, unfeminine, not in the least like women that the media and society kept trying to tell her were doing it right. Mind you, Gemma had seemed to be very much that type of woman, and where had it got her?

She got down on her knees to search under the bed, pulling out more shoe boxes, dust-covered hair clips, old tissues. The tips of her fingers touched something hard and square. She pulled it out – a photograph album. Leafing through it, she could see that the photographs were reasonably recent. Strange, to have a photo album at all – most people used digital albums. The photos were all of Gemma and Nick. *All* of them, Kate realised. Nothing revealing, just everyday shots of the two of them in the office, at various building sites and properties, a couple of party scenes where they shared the same frame. How strange. Poor Gemma must have had a massive crush on her boss. Had it been reciprocated? Was Casey as ignorant of her husband's affairs as he was (as far as Casey knew) of hers? Kate made a mental note to talk to Nick herself and to hell with Anderton if he didn't like it.

There was a photograph near the end of the album that snagged her eye. In it, Gemma and Nick stood side by side, smiling, and on Nick's other side was a woman that after a moment Kate was able to place as Rebecca D'Arcy-Warner. Nick and Gemma were smiling into the camera, full, beaming smiles but Rebecca was looking out of shot and the expression on her face pulled at Kate, nudged her somewhere. It was a look of – what? Misery? Hunger? Something of the two, perhaps. It was an expression she'd seen somewhere before without being able to place it. It made her uneasy - it had a connection with something unpleasant in her memory. With what? She couldn't remember. No doubt it would come back to her. She couldn't tell where the photograph had been taken. The background was blurred – it looked something like a stone wall. She regarded for a moment longer and then shut the album.

Back at the station, Jane and Theo related the findings of their interviews with the neighbours.

"Nothing of great interest," said Jane. She was short and plump, with glorious red curls of the kind you don't see much anymore. *Pre-Raphaelite*, said Kate to herself, watching her talk. What a satisfaction it was to be able to find the right word. What a satisfaction it was to know you were at least adequately educated, even if you'd had to educate yourself.

"Although several people did report seeing a tall man in a Barbour jacket walking towards the house that night," said Theo. "Not actually in Gemma's street, but in the street leading to it. It's probably nothing, but we'll chase it up. Unfortunately it was a bad night, lots of rain and cold so everyone was indoors with the curtains closed."

"We need more background on Gemma Phillips," said Anderton. He turned to Kate. "Would you talk to the people who knew her best? The Fullmans to start with. I'll come with you."

"Yes sir," said Kate, inwardly cheering. Perhaps Anderton had forgiven her for her outburst the previous day.

Nick Fullman opened the front door to them himself. For the first time since Kate had met him, he was dressed casually, in jeans, socked feet and a grey sweatshirt, his dark hair unbrushed, his jaw dark with stubble. He looked stunned, bludgeoned by the knowledge of his assistant's death. Kate wavered a little in her suspicions of him. He looked truly *shocked*, and that was something that was very difficult to fake.

In the kitchen, Nick sat down at the kitchen table. Casey was nowhere to be seen. After a moment, he collected himself and asked whether they wanted coffee.

"I'm not sure where it all is," he said, gesturing to the cupboards. "But if you want one–"

"No, thank you, Mr Fullman." Was the man so babied, so pampered, that he'd never made his own coffee? "We wanted to talk to you about Gemma Phillips, if you feel up to answering some questions? I can see that you've had a shock."

"I have. I can't take it in. Not after everything else. Gemma – I mean, why? Why would someone kill her?" He looked up at them. "She was killed, wasn't she? I mean, I was told she was but – "

"But what, Mr Fullman?"

"I don't know." He shrugged his shoulders. "I thought, it's stupid but perhaps she'd taken Charlie and she – she was so remorseful she'd – you know, killed herself." He looked at their faces. "No, okay, it's a stupid theory."

"I'm afraid there's no doubt that she was murdered, Mr Fullman. Did you really suspect her of having something to do with Charlie's abduction and Dita's death?"

"Well, no – it's just that your mind comes up with all these strange ideas..." He trailed off, running a hand through his messy hair. "I trusted her. I really did trust her, I had to. She had access to everything, all my accounts, business dealings. Like a PA does. That's what I couldn't understand, that I trusted her and yet I still thought – thought she might have done it."

Olbeck and Kate exchanged a glance.

"When did these…suspicions first arise, Mr Fullman?"

"No, you've got it wrong. They weren't really suspicions. I was just thinking – you know – forget I said it. It's really not important now, is it? Not now that this awful thing has happened."

"You weren't angry at her? When you had these ideas?"

"No, and I just said, it wasn't important. It was a throwaway comment, that's all. Just a theory and a pretty stupid one, I know that."

"That's fine, sir," said Olbeck smoothly, as Kate opened her mouth to ask another question. "We're just trying to establish what happened on the night Gemma died. You said she'd asked you for a few days holiday, is that right?"

Nick nodded.

"Yeah. She rings me up and asks for a few days off, doesn't give me any kind of excuse except to say that she just needs a bit of time off after all that's happened."

"Was she in the habit of asking you for time off at short notice?"

"No, she wasn't. She took the odd sick day here and there but she'd never really asked for time off out of the blue for no good reason."

"She'd worked for you for quite a long time, hadn't she?"

Nick shrugged.

"I guess so. A few years."

"So would you say you were close friends? Close colleagues?"

Nick stared as if they'd asked him the name of Gemma's first pet or favourite shade of blue. "I suppose so," he said, after a moment.

"Can you tell us about her? One of the things we try and do is construct a picture of the victim, their likes and dislikes, their history, family and friends and so forth. Can you help us with that sort of thing?"

"Well..."

"It would be a great help to us if you could."

"Well, I'll try," said Nick Fullman. His mouth twisted. "I need Gemma for this. She'd know what to do." His voice thickened and he stopped talking for a second, pinching the bridge of his nose hard. "Sorry, I just–"

"Take a moment if you need one, sir," said Anderton. Kate drummed her fingers on her knees impatiently.

Nick took a deep breath and sat back. "Gemma's thirty-five, I think. *Was* thirty-five. She didn't like celebrating her birthday much, I can't even remember when it was, around June, I think."

"Was she a good secretary?"

"Pretty good. I mean, she could be a little bit lazy sometimes, and she clearly didn't have anything like I do invested in the business – by that I mean it wasn't important to her, not really. I could see that it was just a job to her, but she was okay."

"You two spent long hours working together, didn't you?" asked Kate.

Nick looked at her narrowly.

"Yes."

Kate hesitated, not sure whether to get this personal just yet. Would Anderton head her off? She made up her mind to go ahead. "Long hours and close working conditions can mean that people get, well, more involved with one another than they might do normally."

Nick was still staring at her.

"And?" he said.

"Was there ever anything more between you and Miss Phillips than an employer/employee relationship?"

"Why the hell would you ask that?"

"Could you please answer me, sir?"

Nick dropped his eyes to the table.

"Of course not," he said. "I'm a married man, for a start."

So what? Since when had marriage vows ever stopped anybody? She thought for a second of a name she'd left in the past long ago, the silly sixteen-year-old it had belonged to. Had marriage vows stopped that teenager from doing what she did? She cleared her throat.

"There was never anything between you at all?"

"I said no, didn't I?" said Nick, irritably. He looked at her and she realised he disliked her as much as she disliked him. Anderton raised a placatory hand.

"Thank you, sir. My colleague is just trying to ascertain the facts. One thing we do need to know is what you were doing on the night of Gemma's death."

If the question about an alleged affair hadn't shaken Nick Fullman, this one did. He sat back in his chair, blinking.

"You can't seriously suspect me of – of this. What are you saying?" He was gripping the table with both hands. "You're not serious?"

Anderton attempted to soothe him. "It's routine, Mr Fullman, you must know that. We have to ask everyone connected with the case to establish their whereabouts at the time of the crime."

Slowly, Nick relaxed his grip on the table. He sat back, flexing his fingers a little. His hands shook.

"Fine, fine, I see that," he muttered. "It just gave me a shock."

"So can you confirm your whereabouts between the hours of seven pm and one am on the night of January twenty-fourth?"

"I was..." he began, and then apparently had to

stop and think. "I was at the office. I had to work late. It was flat out, particularly as Gemma hadn't been there that day. I couldn't believe she'd just left me to get on with it. I couldn't *believe* it. Oh God–" He clearly recollected what had happened to his absent assistant. "I didn't mean...anyway, I was at work. In the office."

"Can anyone corroborate that? Did you speak to anyone? Did anyone call in to see you?"

Fullman thought for a moment. "I'm not sure. I – wait, I did make a few phone calls. I–" He stopped talking suddenly.

"Who did you speak to?" There was silence. "Mr Fullman?"

"No one in particular," said Nick, reluctantly.

"Come now, Mr Fullman. Who did you speak to?"

"Um, a friend of mine on the Council. We're friends..."

"Would this be Councillor Gary Jones?"

Fullman looked shocked. "Yes, how did you know?"

"Never mind that now. You spoke to Gary Jones at what time?"

"I don't know, I can't remember. It was late, after nine."

"A strange time to be making a business call," said Kate, earning herself a glare from Nick Fullman.

"It might be to you, Sergeant, but not to me. Besides, it was a personal call, not a business call."

"That's fine, said Anderton, seeing that Kate was about to speak. "The telephone company can provide us with details of your calls." Fullman shifted in his seat again. "We can also confirm your conversation with Councillor Jones himself."

There was a moment of silence in the kitchen, an oddly loaded period of quiet. Then Anderton spoke again. "If you have anything else to tell us, Mr Fullman, I suggest you do so now."

Nick Fullman looked frightened. Kate was reminded of what Rebecca D'Arcy-Warner had said. *Underneath it all, he's just a scared, uncertain little boy...*

"Is there anything you have to tell us, Mr Fullman?" repeated Anderton.

"No," said Nick Fullman, almost inaudibly. Then he said it again, in a firmer voice. "No, there's not."

Chapter Fourteen

OLBECK WAS SURVEYING THE SLIPPING piles of paperwork on his desk with dismay when the desk phone rang, almost hidden under a pile of reports. He pushed the paper to one side, cursing as several folders crashed to the floor, and lifted the receiver.

"DS Olbeck."

The voice on the other end of the phone was quiet.

"I don't want to give my name."

"Fine. How can I help you?"

It was a man's voice, oddly furtive.

"Did you get my note? About Councillor Jones?"

Olbeck mentally sat up straighter.

"We did. Do you have some further information for us, sir?"

There was a moment's hesitation. Then the anonymous voice spoke again.

"Ask Councillor Jones about contaminated land and building on it. Ask Nick Fullman about his new development."

"Can you be more spe–" began Olbeck and then there was the click and burr of a broken connection. He regarded the buzzing handset for a second before replacing it.

"What is it?" said Kate, who had been listening alertly from the other side of the desk.

"The plot thickens. I'll tell you in the car. Come on, we're going to do some digging."

Kate raised her eyebrows.

"Not literally, I hope."

"You never know."

Olbeck drove to Wallingham, pulling up on the edge of a building site. Kate stared through the windscreen at the activity going on: the hauling of bricks, the earth movers, the scaffolding.

"I didn't think you were serious about the digging."

Olbeck grinned. "Don't worry, I just wanted to have a look."

"What is this?" asked Kate, pretty sure she knew the answer.

"Nick Fullman's new development," said Olbeck. Kate nodded. "This is the main project he's working on at the moment."

"Right," said Kate. "And your anonymous caller believes that this land is actually contaminated?"

"That's what they said."

"Contaminated with what?"

"I have no idea."

"Where's their evidence?"

"For all I know, they have none. It could be complete fantasy. Or a personal vendetta against Gary Jones. Or Nick Fullman."

Kate sighed. "So where do we go from here?"

Olbeck took his notebook out of his pocket and started writing.

"We get samples taken for evidence of contamination. If there's something dodgy, then we've got something to go on. We can start questioning people."

"We need to question them anyway. Gary Jones, Nick Fullman and those brothers. How do they tie up with this?"

Olbeck tapped his pen against the steering wheel. "They freely admit to *knowing* Nick Fullman. But I agree with you. They're in this somewhere. The question is, is it actually relevant to the kidnapping and the murders? Or is it just coincidence?"

Kate put her hands in her pockets, hunching her shoulders against the chill wind. She watched the excavators pushing mounds of earth up from a gigantic hole dug in the ground. Pallets of bricks and concrete blocks were stacked up against the chain link fence, and she saw the yellow mass of a digger move slowly along behind the makeshift barrier.

"Let's organise the samples," she said, eventually. "And see where that takes us."

"I'll get Theo to do it. Come on, it's freezing, let's go back."

THE NEXT DAY KATE FOUND herself driving towards Essex, visor tipped down against the winter sun. She found Mr Fullman Senior's place without much drama, pulling into the driveway of a much-extended Thirties house and slotting the car behind a large, black Range Rover.

The woman who answered the door was the person she'd spoken to on the phone. Evie Fullman was John Fullman's second wife, a fact she appraised Kate of almost as soon as she was in the door.

"Oh, no, I'm his step-mother, love," she said, ushering Kate though to the kitchen and perching on one the stools by the breakfast bar. "John's first wife died young, not long after Nick was born, poor soul. He felt it, you know. Well, you would, wouldn't you?" She hopped off her stool and stood poised by the kettle. "Tea?"

"Yes, please. Thank you for seeing me, Mrs Fullman."

"Ooh, call me Evie, please. It's no problem. Anything I can do to help. I can't sleep for thinking of poor Charlie, you know. That poor little mite." She turned her head away sharply, looking at the boiling kettle as if it fascinated her. "Anyway, what was it you wanted to know?"

Kate had heaved herself rather awkwardly up onto a stool.

"I wanted to know about Nick, Mrs Fullman – Evie. Nick and Casey. Presumably you've known Nick for some years? When did you and Mr Fullman marry?"

Evie pursed up her lips, pouring the tea with skill.

"Now that would be telling. All of – ooh, twenty years or so, now. Gawd, doesn't that make me sound ancient?" She handed Kate a mug of tea and hopped up onto her perch again. There was something very birdlike about her: she was a small woman, bosomed like a pigeon, her hair teased into a brittle beehive. Kate felt there was something familiar about her and after a moment, it came to her. Evie reminded her of her mum, except with an added dash of vigour and intelligence and, let's face it, she probably wasn't a piss-head.

"Tea all right, love?" said Evie, with her head on one side.

"Lovely, thanks," said Kate. "So you've known Nick since he was a little boy? You said he was badly affected by his mother's death?"

Evie nodded. "Yes he was. Well, you would be, wouldn't you? There's nothing like your own mother, is there?" Kate winced. "He felt it badly, and I don't believe John really knew how to handle it, to be honest. Well, he's a man, what are you going to do? You didn't talk feelings in them days, not really. "

"How do you and Nick get on?"

Evie eyed her. "Fine, love, as far as I know. We don't see him very often."

"Sorry, I meant more – how did you get on in his childhood? Did he resent his father marrying again?"

That was probably slightly too personal a question, but Kate thought she'd chance it.

"Oh, right you are. Well, it's funny you should say that because you'd have thought that he'd be one to be very jealous. But he wasn't. I think he was quite pleased to have a step-mum. He said as much to me, one day. Made me well up, that did."

"You thought he'd be jealous? Is he a jealous type of person?"

Evie nodded. "He's very intense, love. Always has been. He feels things – and when he was a little boy, he didn't mind showing it. He and his Dad..." She paused for a second to take a sip of cooling tea. "His dad's very old school. He's proud of Nick, of course he is, but they ain't got much in common anymore. Makes them both feel a bit lonely, I think, when they're together."

Kate said nothing, turning her tea cup around in her hands. Then she asked about Casey.

"Nick's wife," she nearly said second wife, "Nick's wife, Casey. How do you get on with her?"

"Me?" Evie raised her eyebrows. "She's a nice girl. Not got a lot to her, to be honest. Not what I'd call a strong personality. That probably suits Nick, though. Always the same with these, what-do-yer-call-em, charismatic men, isn't it? Got little, pretty, quiet wives in the background."

"Would you say it was a happy marriage?"

Evie laughed and then looked sober. "Gawd, I shouldn't be laughing, not with how things are. But, just thinking about it, yes, it seems happy enough for two people who've only been married a year." She winked. "Get to twenty years and then ask me, love, that's when you can say it was happy or not."

Kate smiled. She was thinking that if she were Nick Fullman, she'd have been quite pleased to have this woman for a stepmother too.

"He was with his previous girlfriend for a long time, wasn't he?" she commented.

"Rebecca?"

"Yes," said Kate.

There was a slight change in the atmosphere, almost too subtle for Kate to notice but it was there, just the slightest chill in the air. She mentally sat up a little, alert.

"Rebecca," repeated Evie. She hopped back off her stool and went to the counter, hand poised over the kettle. "More tea, love?"

"No, thanks," said Kate. "Can you tell me anything about Rebecca D'Arcy-Warner?"

Evie had her back turned, busying herself with the kettle.

"Oh, she was a nice girl too," she said. The unspoken "but" hung in the air.

"But?" said Kate.

Evie turned back around to face her. Behind her, the kettle threw clouds of steam into the air.

"Well, for starters, she was a bit out of Nick's league, wasn't she?" Not waiting for an answer, she went on. "She was a cut or five above him, I'd say, and it showed. He felt that, too. Not so much when they were together but when they came here...or saw his old friends..." She trailed off, regarding the teapot blankly. "I always thought there was something a bit...oh, well, it doesn't matter now."

"What do you mean, Evie?"

"Oh, nothing really."

Kate hesitated, wondering whether to push it. Then Evie went on.

"She wasn't a happy girl. Well, woman. No, that she wasn't. That family – well, there were a few stories about her people, posh as they were."

"What do you mean?"

Evie pulled herself back onto her stool, slowly.

"Perhaps it's like that with all those old families," she said, settling herself. "They go back so far, there's always a few who are not quite right."

Kate mentally shook her head.

"Would you say Rebecca, then, was 'not quite right?' Is that what you're trying to say?" Evie said nothing for a moment. Kate persisted. "I know I sound really nosy, but it could be important. Evie?"

Evie pulled out a packet of cigarettes from her cardigan pocket. Without answering, she lit one with a pink plastic lighter and regarded the blue coil of smoke rising slowly from the tip.

"I'm not sure," she said, reluctantly. "It's just something that Nick said once. She'd had some sort of breakdown. Mentally, I mean."

"When?"

"Ooh, I don't know."

"When he was with her? Or afterwards?"

"I'm not sure."

"Was it serious?" Kate wondered whether this was relevant or not. Was she wise to keep pushing for information?

"I don't know, love and that's the truth." Evie gazed at her, blandly, her bouffant head cocked to one side.

"Well..." said Kate, hesitatingly.

"He wasn't kind to her," said Evie, suddenly. She tapped non-existent ash from her cigarette into the ashtray.

"Who wasn't? Nick?"

"I mean, I'm fond of him but even I could see

he wasn't kind. Told him too, I did. Never did hold back with giving my opinions."

"You're saying Nick wasn't kind to Rebecca?" Kate checked. "In what way? Was he abusive toward her?"

Evie's eyebrows went up. "Nick? Gawd, no. Not like *that*. I meant, it wasn't kind of him to keep her hanging on like that."

"How do you mean?"

"Well, girls can say they're not interested in getting married, but you show me one who really isn't. They can say it all they like but they don't fool me."

Kate shifted a little.

"Some women really don't want to get married," she said stiffly.

Evie gave her a wry look.

"Righto. I don't buy it myself. Even the gay ones want to get married nowadays, don't they?"

Kate refused to be sidetracked by this interesting side issue. "Rebecca and Nick were together for a long time. They did get engaged."

Evie snorted. "Engaged, yes, but what does that mean? She was pushing for something more, and Nick threw that her way to keep her happy. Didn't mean it was ever going to actually *happen*."

"And it didn't," said Kate, almost to herself. She was thinking hard. "Rebecca said that her relationship with Nick fizzled out, that they both realised it was for the best when they split up. Do you think that was the case?"

Evie shrugged. "Love, when you get to my age you realise you don't know much about other people's relationships. All I know is what I said to Nick. That girl wanted to get married and you kept her hanging on for it. That's not kind."

"And how did he react when you said that?"

Evie looked uncomfortable. "He laughed." There was a moment's silence. "He didn't mean it to be cruel. He just didn't see what he'd done wrong."

Kate nodded.

"How is he with Charlie?" she asked, switching tack.

Evie looked wary. "What do you mean?"

Kate smiled, trying to put her at her ease. "Is he a hands-on dad, would you say? Was he excited to be a father?"

Evie stubbed out her cigarette. She hopped down from her stool once more and began to to wash up her tea cup, slowly rinsing it under the tap.

"I suppose so," she said, over the noise of rushing water. "It's hard when they're tiny babies though, isn't it? Men don't really get it. They're all for their mums, then, aren't they? Dads aren't really needed."

"Would you say he'd bonded with the baby?"

"Bonded?"

"Yes. Was he affectionate with Charlie? Did he–" Kate stopped herself. "Does he love him?"

Something of Evie's vivacity dimmed a little. She had a tea towel in her hands and she folded it very exactly, lining up the edges and hanging it over the back of one of the kitchen chairs. Kate had the feeling she was stalling for time.

"He was fine with him," she said, shortly. "As fine as he needed to be. There wasn't much he could do with him, was there, Charlie being so young. They just want their mums at that age." Kate flinched, unable to help herself.

There was a moment's silence. Kate knew she should keep questioning Evie, knew she should delve deeper into this line of enquiry, but she was suddenly taut with pain and she didn't think she could trust her voice.

Driving away from the house, uncomfortably full of tea, Kate heard the buzz of an incoming text message on her mobile. She pulled over and checked it. It was from Jay, her younger half-brother, one of her mother's second family and her favourite sibling. Smiling, she opened up the message to find the smile dropping from her face. *Sis, pls call me. Mum in hosp. J xx* read the text.

Kate leant her head against the steering wheel for a moment, swearing softly. This wasn't the first time she'd received news like this. The first time had had her tearing to the hospital in question, even running a red light on the way, such was her hurry.

She'd virtually sprinted to the ward to find her mother fast asleep in a hospital bed and apparently undamaged except for the reek of whisky fumes that permeated her clothes. *Shame they don't have drunk tanks in hospitals*, Kate had hissed furiously to her when she finally woke up.

Now, she just *knew* it would be something similar. She battled with her conscience for a moment and then texted Jay. *Anything serious? Am flat out at wrk. Let me know, K xx.* She drove on, listening out for the chime of an incoming text, hoping against hope that she wouldn't hear it.

Chapter Fifteen

"GOT SOMETHING YOU MIGHT FIND interesting," said Olbeck the next morning, waving a handful of paper under Kate's nose. She looked up from the screen of her mobile – Jay had finally texted her back. *Broken ankle. Sis CALL ME pls x.* She sighed.

"What's up?"

She shook her head. "Nothing that can't wait. What am I going to find interesting?"

Olbeck drew up a chair and fanned the papers out in front of her. "Soil samples from the Wallingham site."

Kate raised her eyebrows. "That was quick. And?"

"It was only quick because apparently the lab had already had several samples posted to them – anonymously. So when our environmental scientist sent ours through, they matched them up pretty quickly."

"Someone had already sent some through?"

Olbeck nodded. "Probably our mystery caller, don't you think?"

Kate bent over the papers.

"I can't make heads nor tails of this," she said after a moment. "Is it contaminated, or isn't it?"

Olbeck grinned. "Once you get past the geek speak, I think the consensus is that although it's nothing too drastically poisonous, the general opinion is that planning permission should not have been granted without, shall we say, some heavy decontamination of the land involved."

"And I assume that hasn't happened?"

"Nope."

"Hmm."

Theo walked over, having clearly overheard what they were discussing.

"Another thing," he said, perching on the side of the desk and knocking over Kate's empty mug. "Whoops, sorry. Anyway, I was doing a bit more digging back into the building regs and paperwork for the site, and guess whose subsidiary company comes up as a part-backer of the development?"

Kate struck a dramatic pose, hand to her forehead. "Could it possibly be...the Costa brothers' company by any chance?"

Theo grinned. "Got it in one."

Olbeck and Kate exchanged glances. Olbeck looked excited but Kate was surprised at her own lack of interest. She had played along with her colleagues, who were clearly pleased at their discovery. but beneath the surface, she was thinking, *So what? That's not it, that's not why this happened.*

Olbeck picked up on her lack of enthusiasm. "What's the problem?"

"Nothing," she said. She didn't want to say anything, given that her misgivings were based purely on instinct. "It's a good lead. Where to from here?"

"You finally get to have the pleasure of the Costa brothers."

"Fabulous. I can hardly wait."

The first and older Costa brother, Stelios Costa, lived in exactly the kind of house that Kate was anticipating: huge, new, brash, vulgar. After a ten minute standoff at the security gates, these were finally swung back by invisible, electronic means, and Olbeck drove slowly onto the forecourt of the house, parking beside an enormous silver Range Rover. *Anyone thinking that crime doesn't pay is wrong in the most literal way, unfortunately,* thought Kate, and she got out of the car feeling cross.

Stelios Costa was standing by the front door of the house, arms folded, watching the two officers approach him. He was a big, powerfully built man, running a little too fat, dressed casually in jeans and a navy hooded sweatshirt. He was smiling, although not by much. He looked Kate up and down in an appraising manner as they came close and she quickly put on a bored expression, to disguise the annoyance she felt.

"Officers," said Stelios as they came to halt in front of him.

"May we come in, sir?" said Olbeck, flashing his warrant card.

"Put that away, Officer Olbeck , I know who you are. And no, you may not come in without a warrant, and I doubt you've got one of those, have you love?"

He addressed this last remark to Kate, who mentally drew an imaginary truncheon and battered him over the head with it. In reality, she smiled slightly and insincerely.

"We have a few questions to ask you–"

Stelios sighed theatrically and cast up his eyes. "I know nothing about the Nick Fullman case, I have no comment, I have nothing to say."

"Interesting that you knew we were going to ask you about Nick Fullman," said Olbeck.

Stelios sneered. "Of course you were. And I may as well tell you now, as I told you before, that we do know him. We are part-backers of his new project in Wallingham. That's in the public domain."

"So you've got nothing to hide."

"That's right."

Kate smiled, or at least widened her mouth. "Is the knowledge that planning permission for those flats was granted despite the land being contaminated in the public domain as well?" she asked. *Take that, you arrogant bastard.*

Stelios looked at her steadily. "Now where did you hear a thing like that?" he asked. A slight shift in his stance made Olbeck take a protective step closer to Kate.

"It's what we know, *sir*," she said, with what she hoped was just the right amount of calculated insolence. "We have samples proving contamination."

Stelios looked at her a moment longer. Then he shrugged. "I have nothing to say, officers," he said. "Talk to the council. It's nothing to do with me."

"You have nothing to say on the matter?"

"I've got nothing to say. That sounds like a council matter to me. If you want to question me further, you can talk to my lawyer."

Olbeck and Kate exchanged a silent glance. They both knew it was pointless going on. The only way they could put the pressure on would be by arresting the man, and they had no grounds to do that.

"We may need to talk to you again, sir," said Olbeck, in a vaguely threatening tone. Stelios looked amused.

"I'll look forward to it," he said. He watched them walk away. Kate just knew he was grinning broadly behind their backs.

Back in the car, they looked at one another.

"Now what?" said Kate.

Olbeck shrugged and started the engine. "We'll dig into it. Talk to the council. Get that slimy bugger Gary Jones to sweat a little."

"You think he's been taking back-handers?"

"I do. But it's not really our concern. That's a matter for the Fraud boys and for the council."

"Mmm."

Kate watched the road slip away beneath the windscreen, the white lines in the centre of the road merging into one long, light strip in her vision.

"I'm going to talk to Fullman," she said, eventually.

Olbeck glanced over. "I wouldn't."

"I think he needs to start talking a bit more than he has."

They drew into the station car park. Olbeck drew the car to a standstill.

"I wouldn't," he repeated. "Let Anderton take the lead."

Kate sat still for a moment, chewing her lip. Then she grabbed her bag and slid from the seat. "I'll risk it," she said. "I won't be long."

Olbeck sighed and handed over the car keys.

"New girl," he said. "Too bloody keen by half."

Kate winked. "It'll wear off soon enough."

She slammed the driver side door, adjusted the seat and drove off, tipping him a salute as she drove past. She could see him in her rear view mirror as she waited to join the main road, shaking his head slowly.

REFUSING TO LISTEN TO THE small voice inside her that was telling her not to be so hasty, she drove to Nick Fullman's office in Wallingham, negotiating the unfamiliar one-way system. Wallingham was a large market town, much developed over the past century and was currently bustling with shoppers, office workers and mothers pushing buggies. Kate averted her eyes from these last whenever she could. She parked the car in the spare parking space outside the offices, smoothed her hair, checked her warrant card and phone and got out.

She hadn't called ahead, but he was in, of course he was. Mrs Bright must be sitting with Casey – or had he left her on her own? She flashed him a big, bright smile.

"Good morning, Mr Fullman. Are you able to answer a few questions for me?"

She pressed forward as she spoke, and he fell back, allowing her into the building.

"I'm surprised to find you at work, sir," Kate said, unable to help one little dig.

Fullman scowled. "As you know, Detective Sergeant, I'm a busy man. Now with Gemma gone, I'm twice as busy. Will this take long?"

"I hope not, sir." Kate found herself a black

leather chair opposite Fullman's mahogany desk and seated herself without waiting to be asked. There was a moment's silence. Nick Fullman sat down opposite her, his brows drawn down. He wore one of his expensive suits and a snowy-white shirt, but his eyes were ringed with shadow and he was unshaven. Kate wondered how much sleep he'd been getting over the past few weeks. Not a lot, by the look of him. Kate mentally shuffled the topics that she had to question him about and picked the first and hopefully least contentious.

"Can you tell me about your relationship with Rebecca D'Arcy-Warner, Mr Fullman?"

Nick Fullman had clearly not been expecting this. His eyebrows went up.

"Rebecca?" he said. "What about her?"

"I understand that you had a very long term relationship with her."

"Yes. And?"

"Why did you split up?"

"Why do you want to know? What possible relevance can it have?"

"Please just answer my question, sir. Why did you split up?"

Nick stared at her. "We just grew apart," he said, stonily.

"There was no other reason?"

"What do you mean?" He didn't wait for her to answer. "What has she said?"

Kate took the plunge. "She mentioned that you'd been keeping what she called 'reprehensible company.' The Costa brothers? Rebecca said she didn't approve."

Nick's eyes bulged. "What? She said that?"

"Is it true?"

"I – I–" he blustered for a moment and then sat forward, putting his large hands on the desk. Kate was reminded rather uneasily of his physical presence. "I have met them, yes. That's all. They own a lot of property. That's all. That's how I met them."

"You don't have any business dealings with them?"

"Well–"

"You haven't, for example, been involved in one of their latest building projects?"

Nick stared at her. "What do you mean?"

"I mean the latest development of new-build flats in Wallingham, Mr Fullman. The development built on brownfield land. The development that was apparently granted permission despite being on contaminated land?"

Nick's hands were shaking. They both looked at them before he removed them from the desk and tucked them out of sight.

"I don't know what you're talking about," he said, feebly.

"You don't, sir? Despite your close friendship

with Councillor Jones? Councillor Jones who heads the planning department and has final say over permission granted for new buildings?"

Nick seemed to recollect himself.

"So what?" he said, sitting up a little straighter. "If there's a problem with the planning permission, you should be talking to the council, not to me. It's nothing to do with me."

"Isn't it?"

"No."

"Your development of flats, sir. The Costa brothers are part-backers of the project, isn't that right?"

There was a moment's silence. Nick turned his face away from her. "I have nothing to say on that matter, officer."

Kate itched to arrest him. She opened her mouth to start the words of the caution, thought again, shut it. She didn't know why, but she suddenly knew that the contaminated land issue wasn't the reason for Charlie's disappearance. Anderton would scoff, but she *knew*. She remembered Charlie's little face in the magazine, so tiny and vulnerable. She thought of Mrs Bright and Evie, both mothers and grandmothers, and the words they'd both used to describe Nick. *Jealous, difficult, resentful...* His child was gone and had he even wanted him in the first place? Hot, bitter anger suddenly rose up in her, almost choking her. She couldn't keep the words back any longer.

"Do you *want* us to find your son, sir?"

Nick's head whipped around to face her again. He looked stunned.

"What do you mean? Of course I do."

"Do you, sir?"

"Yes!"

Kate looked him directly in the eye. "Do you want us to find your son, sir?"

Nick put his hands on the desk again and leaned forward. "Are you mad? What do you mean by that?"

Kate spoke quietly. "You've not bonded with your son, sir, have you? You hired a nanny to take care of him from birth. You kept him in a nursery way away from your bedroom. You've never changed his nappy or fed him or taken care of him yourself, have you, sir? Why is that? Do you resent him?" Nick was staring, aghast.

Kate felt the words coming out of her mouth, unable to stop the torrent of accusation. "You didn't want him, did you, sir? You were jealous of him, weren't you? Jealous of a baby screaming all the time, waking in the night, getting all the attention, all the attention that should have been yours? What happened that night, Nick? Did it all get too much for you? Did you–"

"That's enough!" Nick Fullman was on his feet, facing her across the table, shaking. Kate found herself on her feet too. Her legs felt as though they were going to collapse beneath her.

"How dare you, how dare you–" Nick tripped over the words. "Get out of here. Get out!"

Kate recollected herself. What the hell had just happened there? She attempted to say something, something placatory.

Nick Fullman was coming around the desk. She flinched, unable to help herself. He stopped a few feet away, staring at her with loathing. "Get out," he said, quietly and with menace.

"Sir–"

"Now!"

She backed away until she was at the door, and then turned, trying not to scurry. She could barely hear anything over the thump of blood in her ears. She reached the car, fumbled for the keys, dropped them, bent to pick them up, dropped them again. When she was finally in the driver's seat, she sat for a moment, swallowing convulsively.

What the hell, Kate? You idiot, she told herself in fury. *What have you done?* Through the window of the office, she could see Nick Fullman pick up the phone, and the dread and sickness inside her leapt up another notch.

Chapter Sixteen

BACK AT THE OFFICE, SHE went to the women's toilets and stood for a moment, regarding her face in the mirror. That last scene with Nick Fullman replayed itself in her head. What had she *done*? She'd virtually accused him of murdering his own son. She thought of Anderton saying 'get the evidence' and winced. What evidence did she have, apart from her own dislike of the man? For a moment she thought she was going to be sick.

There was that awful hollow feeling inside, the *I've fucked up badly* feeling. A feeling she hadn't had for years, not since she'd looked at the blue line on a pregnancy test at age sixteen and realised, with a wave of horror and misery washing over her, that she had just ruined her life. And here she was, years later, ruining her life again.

Kate ran the cold taps over her wrists. Perhaps it would be okay. Perhaps Fullman wouldn't do anything. *Fuck, please don't let him do anything*. She pulled a paper towel from the dispenser and dried her hands. Then she pinned a neutral expression to her face and went back to the office. Through the inner window, she could see Olbeck put the phone on his desk back down with a bang, soundless through the glass. Then he threw the pencil he was holding across the desk. She squared her shoulders, took a deep breath and went into the room.

Olbeck didn't look up at her arrival.

"You all right?" said Kate, pleased that her voice sounded so normal.

"Fine." He looked a little ashamed of the abruptness of his answer. "Domestic dramas. As usual. How was it? Get anything useful?"

I accused Nick Fullman of the murder of his son. Virtually. On no evidence. Kate mentally shook herself. She wasn't going to mention anything about the conversation – the argument – that she'd just had with Fullman. What could she say? She recollected her talk with Evie, a million years ago, it now seemed.

"Nick Fullman's a jealous commitment-phobe who kept his last girlfriend hanging on waiting for marriage and drove her mad in the process. Apparently."

Olbeck winced.

"What's wrong?"

"Nothing. "

"Anderton wants an update."

Kate felt her stomach drop. "Now?"

182

"Yes. You have to see him the second you get in, apparently."

Kate slung herself into her chair. "Great." She swallowed down the nausea that was rising fast. "I'll go right away."

Olbeck stared at her. "Are *you* all right?"

Well, I'm about to be utterly bollocked. If not fired.

"I'm fine," said Kate shortly, and left the room.

Anderton was seated at his desk when Kate walked into his office. This was the first time she'd seen him in a stationary position since she'd known him, and from this she realised that she was in very deep trouble indeed. She closed the door behind her, noting with detached interest that her legs were actually shaking. She wasn't sure whether to sit down, but she didn't want to fall over in a heap.

"Sit down," said Anderton briefly, and Kate subsided gratefully into a chair.

"I expect you know why you're here," he went on. Kate opened her mouth to say something, and he raised a hand, silencing her.

There was a moment of quiet.

"Do you remember me saying at the start of this investigation that I didn't want anyone steaming in, upsetting people with their own clumsy prejudices?"

Kate swallowed.

"Yes, sir."

"So why, in fact, have you done just that when I expressly asked you not to?"

Kate's heartbeat thumped in her ears. She gripped the sides of her chair. "Sir, I–"

"You are a police officer, DS Redman. You work on evidence. Where is your evidence for accusing Nick Fullman of the murder of his child and his nanny?"

Kate closed her eyes briefly. She could actually feel sweat beading on her upper lip.

"Sir, I'm sorry–"

"Do you realise the damage it does to a case when accusations are flung around with no evidence to back them up? Do you want to further jeopardise the safety of a vulnerable baby because of your own emotional issues?"

Kate's heart was thumping.

"No, I'm sorry, sir. I can't tell you how sorry I am." Anderton didn't say anything for a moment, and she pressed on. "You must admit that we have to at least look at the possibility that Nick Fullman is inv–"

Anderton's shout and bang of his hand on his desk made her jump.

"Do you not think that that's been in the back of my mind since this case began, Detective Sergeant? Do you not think that perhaps the reason we haven't moved forward on that assumption is that there is simply *no evidence*? If Nick Fullman is guilty, do you want to see the case thrown out by the CPS at the first hurdle because we haven't got a single scrap of evidence with which to charge him? Do you?"

Kate could feel tears pressing at the back of her eyes. *Don't cry, Kate, whatever you do, don't cry.* She dug her fingernails into her legs.

"No, sir." She wanted to say something more but at that second, she couldn't trust her voice.

Anderton sat back in his chair, exhaling. There was a moment's silence, during which Kate tried to breathe normally.

Then Anderton sat forward.

"You're a promising officer, DS Redman. I had excellent reports of you from Bournemouth. You'll go far, I have no doubt."

Kate blinked. "Thank you, sir."

"I should tell you, though, that I had serious doubts about allowing you onto this case."

Kate held her breath, knowing he was about to say more.

"I had serious doubts because of the nature of the case and because of, shall we say, your personal history."

Kate looked across the table. Anderton was sitting very still, his hands on the desk in front of him. She felt pinned to her chair by his eyes. Her heart began thumping so heavily she was surprised it wasn't audible to the grim-faced man sat opposite her.

"What do you mean, sir?" she said, cursing the feebleness of her voice. Why was she asking, anyway? She didn't know what the answer was, but she was damn sure she wouldn't like it.

Anderton spoke quietly.

"I knew you would find this case an emotive one, DS Redman, because you yourself had a baby taken from you at roughly Charlie Fullman's age."

Kate said nothing for a moment. For a second, she thought she was going to be sick.

Anderton was still speaking.

"I'm sorry to remind you of what was no doubt a painful time for you, DS Redman, but I'm sure you can appreciate my concerns and more particularly now in the light of recent developments."

"He wasn't taken away," said Kate, hoarsely.

"I'm sorry?"

"My – the baby. He wasn't taken away."

"No, that's true. You gave him up for adoption, didn't you?"

Kate nodded, mutely, unable to speak. She wanted to ask, *How did you know*? but of course it would be in her notes, on her profile.

Don't cry, Kate. Don't cry.

Anderton was regarding her silently. She felt flayed, her skin raw and prickling with shock. This was the nightmare come to life, the thing she'd been dreading since that last meeting with the adoption agency twelve years ago. She wanted to get up and walk out of the office, but she couldn't trust her legs.

"It must have been very painful for you," said Anderton eventually, quietly. Kate couldn't even nod for fear of dislodging the tears that were trembling on the edge of her eyelids.

"I don't know if you've ever had counselling..." he said, watching her. She managed to shake her head, carefully. She couldn't have stood any type of counselling – having to sit there and pull all those painful memories back out again, having to face up to what she'd done. Instead she'd kept those memories locked up in a box, somewhere deep inside of her. Covered over with dust and locked away.

"Perhaps you should think about it," Anderton said. He sat back in his chair, sighing a little. Kate turned her face up to the ceiling, blinking. Anderton went on. "I want you to go home now, DS Redman. Take the afternoon off. Calm down. Come back tomorrow, and we'll start again."

"Yes, sir," said Kate. She cleared her throat. "Thank you, sir."

She took a deep breath and got up. Anderton raised one finger to stop her.

"One more outburst like that," he said. "And you are off the case. Not just off the case, in fact, off the force. One more. Do I make myself clear?"

Her tears had gone, and this time she managed to nod.

"Yes, sir."

He swung round in his chair, dismissing her.

"Off you go, then."

Chapter Seventeen

KATE CLOSED AND THEN LOCKED the door behind her. She stood for a moment in the hallway of her flat, palms extended slightly, turned outward, trying to drink in the calm that normally descended when she returned home. She breathed in deeply, trying to block out Anderton's words and the memories that those words conjured up.

After five minutes, she realised it wasn't going to be possible. Those words kept reverberating. *You gave him up for adoption, didn't you? You gave him up for adoption, didn't you?* Kate put her hands up to her face. She *would not* cry. She wasn't a crier. She felt the tears brimming. She would not.

She stumbled into the living room, lounge – what the fuck did it matter what she called it? Why was she trying to escape what she was, pretend her past didn't matter, try and be something she wasn't? *That was proper cold, Kelly, it weren't natural.* Her own mother had said that about her. Was it true?

She'd given her baby away. He was gone, taken away, as lost to her as Charlie was to Casey.

No, not that. She'd signed him over. She'd allowed them to take him from her. She saw his face again, the face she saw whenever her defences were down. His little old-man face. He hadn't looked anything like her, apart from his long fingers and his dark curls of hair. She could still remember, twelve years later, the sheer, grinding agony of the labour pains. How it felt as if she was splitting in two. The hoarseness of her voice a day later, from all the screaming. The ache, the misery of every muscle in her body having strained to push her boy out.

Her boy. But he wasn't, was he? At least Casey had had that, had had her Charlie for three months. What had Kelly had, for she was still Kelly then? Her birth name had gone with her baby. And what had she got to show for it? For a second, she saw the future and it was dark and empty.

She'd reached the sofa, and her face was buried in its cushions. Her nails sank into the fabric of the seat. She could see his little face in her mind's eye, right there, pink and crumpled and with that fluffy, dark birth hair. With a gasp of pain, she realised she had no idea what colour his hair would be now. Was he even alive? She groaned into the cushion, mouth agape.

After five minutes, she sat up. Grief battled

against self consciousness. She knelt for a moment, wiping her eyes and hiding her face, as if there was someone else in the room, judging her.

She drifted into the kitchen and switched on the kettle, automatically. Then, disregarding the cup and sachet of camomile tea that she'd prepared, she went into the hallway and looked up at the hatch in the ceiling.

Twenty four minutes later, Kate levered open the dusty lid of the box she'd brought down from the attic. Her fingers shook as she put the box lid aside and lifted out the contents. For a moment, she was ashamed of the thick layer of dust that coated the lid of the box and then thought of how ridiculous that sounded. Even she didn't dust her *attic*, for God's sake.

Here were the scan photos, encased in a twee little envelope with a cartoon picture on the front and a caption in scribbly font that said *My Baby*. He wasn't, though, was he? He hadn't really ever been hers. Kate drew in a breath that was dangerously close to a sob. She took out the first photo, taken at twelve weeks. Twelve weeks from conception and here was a photograph. Even now she found that incredible. Here he was, curled like a bud but still recognisably human. Arms extended, little legs, the unmistakeable bump of his nose and curve of his forehead. Here was the scan at twenty weeks, much more baby-like now. Little skeletal face turned towards the camera. Fingers, toes. He had one hand up to his cheek, as if sleeping. Had he been asleep? Kate remembered the sonographer prodding her swollen belly, trying to get him to move. He had moved, hadn't he? She allowed herself to remember. Twenty weeks and he was a lively one, rolling and kicking and punching her from within.

A teardrop fell onto the scan picture and Kate wiped it away gently. How had she got through nine months of pregnancy knowing that she would lose him? Don't say that, don't say *lose him*, as if it's something that happened accidentally. As if it was nothing to do with you. *You gave him away.* Kate felt a kick in her belly again, as if a phantom baby was protesting within her. How had she gone through nine months of pregnancy without going mad?

You're more malleable when you're young. You're better able to take things. What you lack in wisdom, you make up for in shock absorption. You're like a young tree; you can bend in the storm but you won't break. Kate thought of Courtney, sixteen years old. If Courtney had a baby in the next year, Kate would be horrified. She was a *child*. *As I was*, she thought. *As I was*. What had he been thinking, that man in the pub? What had he been doing, seducing a child? *Come off it, Kate. You loved being taken for someone older than yourself. All teenagers do. You knew what you were doing.*

She wiped her eyes and turned her attention

back to the box. Here was the letter from the hospital, telling her of the miniscule risk of Down's Syndrome for the baby. She'd paid for that test, it hadn't been offered as a routine option. Of course it hadn't, she was only seventeen years old. Why had she paid for it, why had she cared, knowing she wouldn't be keeping the baby anyway? Because she'd wanted to know. He hadn't had Down's Syndrome, anyway. He'd been perfect.

She lifted out the last bundle of papers. These were all from the private adoption agency, all with that distinctive blue and orange logo on the headed paper. It was good quality paper, thick and creamy. Arranging adoptions was obviously a lucrative business. Why had she used a private agency? Because she'd thought that if you had money, you'd make a better parent? She *had* thought that. Kate cringed in shame. *Stupid girl, stupid idiot.*

She looked again at the letters and wondered whether they'd meant the logo to look quite so much like a colourful embryo. Perhaps it was deliberate, reminding all the hopeful, would-be parents of what they couldn't have. The fuckers. She could feel her teeth set in a something that wasn't a grin. Kate felt as if that logo was burned into her retinas, something she'd be seeing every time she closed her eyes at night. She'd probably see it on her death bed. She skimmed through the papers, hesitating over the very last one, a sealed envelope. It was a copy of the letter she'd written to the baby, for him to open on his eighteenth birthday. If his adoptive parents gave it to him, that is. Perhaps they'd burned or torn it up and thrown it away. She picked it up and put it down again. She couldn't read it, not yet. It was too painful.

Why had she kept all of this? Was it because she was afraid to throw away official papers? Did she worry about forgetting? She almost laughed at that, a thin, gaspy wheeze. As if she would ever forget. *I know why I've kept them*, she thought. *It's because I knew one day I'd have to do this. Look through them. Face up to what I've done.*

She put the papers back into the box, neatly, and shut the lid, returning that blue and orange logo to darkness. Then she opened it and took them out again, unable to leave them alone. She went and made herself that camomile tea, but she didn't drink it. She held it to her chest and sat on the sofa and wept, for her lost baby, for her seventeen-year-old self. For all the mistakes she'd made, the regrets of the past and her fears for the future. Wept open-mouthed, tears dropping onto her legs, onto the papers on her lap, marking those official words.

Chapter Eighteen

"YOU ALL RIGHT?" SAID OLBECK, the next morning, noting Kate's red eyes.

"I've got a cold," said Kate. She sniffed. "I'll be fine."

"What did Anderton want?"

"Nothing."

He gave her a wry look. "Really?"

Kate swung her chair away. "I don't really want to talk about it, Mark. Sorry."

"All right. Hey, don't worry, we've all been there. He does this, you know, if you stuff up. Don't take it personally."

Kate turned back to him. "Fine, I won't. Can we leave it now?"

Olbeck raised his hands above his head in a "don't shoot" gesture.

"Leaving it right now." He paused. "Anyway, Anderton wants us to double check alibis for the night of Gemma's death. I'm doing Saheed, but I can do Rebecca Thingy as well if you like."

Kate hesitated. If she took on Rebecca's, it would mean another drive down to Cudston Magna. Could she bear to be in the car by herself for an hour, trapped with her own thoughts? Olbeck was looking at her. She battled with herself and then her conscience won.

"It's all right, I'll do hers," she said, getting up and reaching for her car keys.

It was a beautiful day, the first sunshine for a long time. As Kate waited at a traffic light, she looked at the hedgerow by the car window and saw the first, tiny green buds unfurling. Spring is coming. She felt a little bit better than she had done. *One day, this will all be in the distant past*, she thought, *and perhaps it won't hurt quite as much as it does now*. Twelve years was nothing, it was the blink of an eye. Then it caught her again: her tiny baby boy was now a twelve year old. She caught her breath and blinked hard against the tears, stretching her eyes wide to stop them falling.

The car behind hooted and she realised the lights had changed.

The Georgian manor looked just as imposing as it had the first time. Kate realised as she pulled up outside and parked the car that she hadn't rung ahead to announce her arrival. What was the matter with her? *You're losing it*, she chastised herself. She took a moment to compose herself, sitting behind the steering wheel, smoothing her hair back with one hand.

She rang the doorbell once, waited five minutes, and then rang again. Nobody was home. What a waste of a journey... She was just turning to go back down the steps to her car when the door opened, slowly and hesitantly. Brigadier D'Arcy-Warner stood on the threshold, blinking and peering at her rather like a mole peering out of a burrow.

Kate got out her warrant card.

"Is your daughter in, Mr D'Arcy-Warner?" As she said it, she was suddenly conscious that she'd used the wrong title. "My apologies, um, Brigadier. Is Rebecca in?"

"Rebecca?" said the Brigadier in a puzzled tone.

"Yes, your daughter. Is she here?"

"No," said the Brigadier, after a long moment. He pulled the door open a bit wider. "Do come in, my dear. I'll make you a cup of tea. Do you like tea?"

"Oh no, that's..." Kate realised he'd turned away, leaving the door open. She hesitated for a second and then followed him into the hallway.

The Brigadier plodded slowly across the black and white tiles towards a door at the far end of the hall. As Kate hesitated, he turned back.

"Come here, my dear."

Kate walked across the acres of tiling until she was level with him. He stood, peering at her in the dimness.

"Are you a friend of Rebecca's?"

"I'm a police officer, sir. Is Rebecca here?"

The Brigadier's bushy eyebrows went up. "A policeman, eh? Have you come about the burglary?"

"I'm sorry?"

The Brigadier indicated another door on the right of the corridor. "There's been a burglary," he said. "In the study. Have you come about that?"

Kate hesitated for a second.

"Could you show me, sir?"

The Brigadier led her to a small, wood-panelled study. A desk stood by a window, with drawers akimbo and papers scattered over the surface and drifted onto the floor.

"It's here," said the Brigadier. He regarded the mess for a moment. "I think it was a burglary. It may have been me. I get in a mess sometimes."

Kate sighed inwardly.

"Sir, can you be more specific? Has there actually been a burglary?"

"No," said the Brigadier, sadly. Another mass of paper slipped from the desk to the floor. "It must have been when I was looking for something. It's hard to remember things, sometimes. You'll know that, when you get to my age."

"Yes," said Kate, remembering what Rebecca had said. *He has dementia.* Did he really, though, or was he just old and forgetful? Would he remember whether his daughter had been with him on the night of Gemma's death? Was it even worth asking? *Perhaps I'll be like that when I'm his age and then I'll be happy not to remember everything.*

She opened her mouth to ask the question, but the Brigadier had already started walking towards the door.

"You stay here, my dear," he said. "I'll bring you your tea. I can do that."

Kate began a sentence and then thought better of it. Was he even able to find the kitchen? Where were the live-in carers, the home-helps that Rebecca had mentioned on their first visit? She saw no point in hanging around waiting for the Brigadier to remember how to boil a kettle, but she decided to wait for a moment. He closed the door of the study behind him, leaving Kate in the room.

She stood for a moment and then went to the chair by the desk, moving a mass of papers from the seat to the floor. What a mess. She looked out of the window at a little flowerbed and a slice of lawn. What must it have been like to grow up here? She sat back against the chair, allowing her eyes to drift from the window to the surface of the desk, from the open drawers to the piles of paper on the floor. Then she froze.

There was the logo, the blue and orange logo. The curled, embryonic shape. The logo she'd seen last night, on the paper from the adoption agency. There it was, on a letter on the floor, peeking out from underneath a pile of other letters. Kate leant down, her heart thumping. She knew she hadn't been mistaken, but peering closer confirmed it. It was the same logo. It was a letter from the same adoption agency. She twitched at it and saw the salutation, *Dear Ms. D'Arcy-Warner...*

"Here you go, my dear," said the Brigadier, crashing open the door. Kate jumped and sat upright. He came into the room, balancing a cup on a saucer.

"Tea for you," he said proudly. Kate took it, barely able to mutter her thanks. It was stone cold.

"OLBECK, IT'S ME. I NEED you to get onto the Wenlove Agency. It's an adoption agency, Wenlove Agency, W-E-N-L-O-V-E. Talk to the MD, ask about Rebecca D'Arcy-Warner. It's urgent."

"What the hell? What's happened?"

"Just talk to them. Actually don't, just get me the number. I'll be back in twenty minutes, and I need to talk to them."

Twenty minutes was pushing it, but Kate put her foot down. Damn the speed limits. She wished Olbeck was here, driving, so she could have time to think. What did it mean? Did it mean anything? She remembered Rebecca sitting opposite her, very upright, clasping her ringless fingers together. *I'm not very maternal, I'm afraid.* Had *she* had a child adopted? Kate slid to a stop at a red light, cursing the delay. Should she pull over and call the agency, right now? No, she needed to be in the office. *Come on, come on.* The light changed and she shot forward.

Back at the office, she appraised Olbeck of the situation.

"But how did you know it was the Wenlove's logo?" he asked.

Kate had been dreading this bit.

"I just know," she said, praying he wouldn't ask for more details. "I can't go into it now but I know it, I know it was the logo of a private adoption agency. Just take it from me."

Olbeck nodded.

"Theo pulled up the info. Managing Director is a Graham Winterdown. He pulled the old 'that's highly confidential card' when I spoke to him, until I told him it was a double murder enquiry."

"So he knows we're coming?"

"He does. Come on, I'm driving."

Chapter Nineteen

GRAHAM WINTERDOWN WAS A SMALL, neat man, with a fussy beard and smooth, long-fingered hands. Kate disliked him on sight. Walking through the reception area, she was transported back twelve years, when she'd come here once before to sign the papers. To sign over her boy. She clenched her fists and then consciously forced herself to relax them. She'd made two visits here, one for the paper signing and one more, to meet the prospective parents. The people who would be raising her child. Kate caught her breath in a gasp of pain and then stopped, struck by something that had just occurred to her. The adoptive parents... the woman's face... her train of thought was derailed as they were ushered into the managing director's office.

"This is very irregular," said Winterdown disapprovingly as they sat down in chairs opposite his desk. "I appreciate that you need the information but I'm very worried about the security of our clients' details."

"Any information will be safe with us," said Kate. She took in the luxurious fittings of his office: the mahogany desk, the crystal carafe of water perched on top. On the far wall was a large, black and white photograph of a smiling baby dressed in a pair of striped dungarees.

"What was it you wanted to know?" asked Winterdown after offering refreshments and having them refused.

Olbeck had explained the purpose of their visit during his telephone call. He repeated as much to Winterdown.

"Ah, yes." Winterdown extracted a file from the drawer of his desk. "I just wanted to be sure that I had the facts right, as it were."

Kate longed to arrest him for being a smug, sanctimonious git.

"You've been in correspondence with Rebecca D'Arcy-Warner," she said, sharply. "We need to know why."

Winterdown raised his eyebrows at her tone but didn't comment. He offered the file in his hand to her.

"We did indeed have some correspondence with a Ms D'Arcy-Warner," he said, as Kate took the file. "All of the paperwork relating to the lady is in that file. She applied to us to become an adoptive parent two years ago now."

"And did she become one? An adoptive parent?"

"She did not."

Olbeck and Kate exchanged glances.

"Why not?" said Olbeck.

Winterdown moved a pen into alignment with the edge of his desk.

"There are many reasons someone wouldn't make a suitable adoptive parent," he said, after a moment. "We have very stringent criteria before people are approved to adopt. It's all in the best interests of the children."

"Of course," said Kate. "But can you be more specific? Why was Rebecca turned down? Or did she change her mind?"

"No, she didn't change her mind."

"So you turned her down?"

"We did." He clearly realised he was expected to elaborate. "There were certain...pointers, shall we say, that led us to believe that she was not entirely a – stable person. Not suitable for adopting a child."

"She had a history of mental illness?"

Winterdown looked shocked.

"My goodness me, no, nothing like that. Under interview though, she made several comments that in the light of day seemed inappropriate in an adoptive parent. Anyone who wants to adopt must realise that the whole thing *must* proceed with regard to what's best for the child. Not what's best for themselves."

"She was eager to adopt, though?"

"Very much so."

Kate was riffling through the papers in the file.

"We must take these, Mr Winterdown." Had he overseen her son's adoption? "How long have you worked here?"

"I'm sorry?"

"How long have you been Managing Director here?"

His eyebrows went up again.

"For the last – let me see – six years? Yes, I think it must be six years."

Olbeck was giving her an odd look. She closed the file.

"We'll take this, Mr Winterdown. I'll give you a receipt for it, and you can be assured that we'll be very careful with it."

"You all right?" said Olbeck when they were back in the car.

Kate nodded, brushing at her eyes. She sniffed.

"Still got that cold, I see," he said, in a neutral tone.

They drove for a moment in silence.

"We need to get a warrant to search her house," said Kate. "The mansion and Rebecca's own house."

"Do we have the grounds?"

"I think so. For a start, she's lied to us. You heard her tell us she wasn't maternal yourself. She said children weren't in her game plan, or something like that. And yet, two years ago, she's trying to adopt a child."

"Perhaps that's why she told us that. You know, she gets turned down for adoption and decides that she isn't ever going to be a parent and pretends that's been her plan all along. Protesting too much, you know."

"It's still a lie."

"I know," said Olbeck, indicating to turn off the main road. "I just don't know if it's enough."

"I never did check her alibi for the night of Gemma's death. We need to question her."

"I know. Let's go there now."

He pulled the car over and called the station, asking Theo for her home address and punching it into the sat nav.

While this was happening, Kate was thinking hard. There was something nagging at her, something that was important. Something to do with Gemma. What was it? She scrolled back through her memories, thinking back to the last time she was at Gemma's house. Oh yes, there it was. She opened her mouth to tell Olbeck and shut it again. *Tell him and you'll have to tell him why you know what you do...* Kate battled with herself. *Tell Olbeck and you'll have to tell him everything.* Could she bear for anyone else to know? Anderton knowing was bad enough. But it was important. Kate knew it was important. She made up her mind.

"There's something else," she said, reluctantly, as the car began moving again.

Olbeck glanced over at her.

"Yes?"

"Yes." She took a deep breath, steadying herself. "There's a photograph of Rebecca D'Arcy-Warner at Gemma Phillips' house. In that weird photo album full of photos of Nick Fullman."

"Yes?" said Olbeck, clearly expecting more.

"It's of the three of them together. I'm not sure where it was taken. Rebecca has this look on her face, a very intense expression. It bothered me because I knew I'd seen that exact type of look before, but I couldn't remember where."

"Right," said Olbeck. "And?"

Kate knew she was dragging this out because she didn't want to tell him. *Come on, get a grip.* She took another deep breath. She was trembling.

"When I was seventeen," she began. For a moment, her voice failed. "When I was seventeen, I had a baby adopted."

There it was, the bald statement. Olbeck said nothing but he gave a little whistle of surprise.

"Okay," he said, eventually. They were both looking straight ahead, Olbeck out of necessity, Kate because she didn't want to look at him. She swallowed.

"I'm sorry to hear that," said Olbeck. "That must have been really hard."

Kate tried to say "it was." For a moment, the tears threatened to overcome her. She swallowed again and again.

"It was," she said, when she could trust her voice. "But I'm telling you this for a reason, I don't want to go into too much detail. But the look on Rebecca's face in the picture, it's the same look as the one on the face of the adoptive parents that I met. The woman – the mother – when – when I had my son adopted. She looked just like that. "

There was a moment's silence.

"You're sure?" said Olbeck. He glanced over at her. "I'm really sorry about that, Kate."

"S'okay," said Kate, in a watery voice. She concentrated on breathing in and out. "I am sure, though. I couldn't forget it. The look on her face – the woman's – when she saw the picture of my son."

She pinched the bridge of her nose. "Believe me, it's the same look."

"I believe you. I can't see it helping us much though. I mean, a look is not evidence."

"I know that," snapped Kate, taking emotional refuge in anger. "It's another reason why we have to interview her now, today."

Olbeck checked the sat nav.

"We're almost there. Hold tight."

No one came to answer the door, even after repeated pealing of the doorbell. The house was a semi-detached Edwardian building, handsome and well-kept. Kate peered through the front bay window at a pleasant, tidy sitting room.

"Are you looking for someone?" asked a woman who was walking up the path of the house next door. She was a middle-aged lady with greyish-blonde hair, clothes and accent impeccable.

"Rebecca D'Arcy-Warner," said Kate. "Have you seen her recently?"

"Not for weeks," said the neighbour. "It's funny you ask because I was thinking to myself it's ages since I've seen Rebecca, and I was almost wondering whether she'd moved. Not that she'd have gone without saying goodbye, I'm sure."

"Thank you, Mrs – ?"

"Mrs Smithson, Barbara Smithson." She looked startled at the production of their warrant cards. "Oh dear, there isn't any trouble is there?"

Kate hastened to reassure her. "We're just anxious to have a chat with Ms D'Arcy-Warner," she said. "Are you close friends with her?"

"Well, not especially close, I suppose. We're *friendly*. Well, you have to be, being neighbours, don't you?"

Olbeck stepped forward.

"May we have a word with you, Mrs Smithson? Me and my colleague would like to talk to someone who knows Rebecca, even if it is on a casual basis."

"Rebecca's a very nice person. She would always sign for any parcels if they came while I was out, and when my husband and I went away on holiday last year, she kept an eye on the house for us, watered the plants, that sort of thing."

"So she was a good neighbour?" asked Olbeck, nursing a mug of weak coffee.

"Yes. I mean, I don't know her *well* or anything like that, but she is certainly a very pleasant person."

Kate sat still with difficulty. She felt fizzy with energy, itching to *do* something. What she didn't want to do was sit around drinking yet another hot drink and listening to the meaningless pleasantries of this neighbour. She forced herself to sit still.

"Rebecca's not married, is she?" said Olbeck.

Mrs Smithson shook her head. "No, she's not."

"Does she have a boyfriend? A partner?"

"I wouldn't know. I don't think so. I've not seen her with anyone here."

"Has she had many visitors in the last few weeks that you're aware of?"

Mrs Smithson sat, twisting her hands. "I'm not sure," she said, nervously. "I haven't noticed anyone in particular."

This was useless. Kate tried to beam her thoughts into Olbeck's head. If he wasn't going to make a move soon, she would do it for him. "Well, that's-" she began, standing up, when Mrs Smithson exclaimed.

"Oh, I almost forgot. I took in a parcel for Rebecca myself, not that long ago. That one up there." She indicated a box on the kitchen dresser. "I expected she'd call round for it, but I haven't seen her for so long, I quite forgot about it."

"May I have a look?" said Kate, not waiting for an answer. She lifted the box, shook it and then opened it. Mrs Smithson made a small noise of protest, but by that time, both Olbeck and Kate could see what the parcel contained. It was a baby monitor.

Kate called Anderton as they drove to Cudston Magna. She appraised him of the situation in a few short sentences.

"Good, do just that," he said after she stopped speaking. "Don't go in hard, though. This could be very tricky."

"But I can arrest?"

"Yes, of course. I'm sending Theo and Jerry over as well for back up."

"Thank you, sir."

Chapter Twenty

SHE AND OLBECK DIDN'T SPEAK for the rest of the journey. He was concentrating on driving, and she held onto her knees, gripping tightly to stop her fingers shaking. At last, they were turning down the driveway of the manor house, the gravel making a rushing noise under the wheels. The house looked peaceful, its many windows glittering in the weak spring sunlight.

No one came to the door. Kate tried it and rattled the door handle.

"Locked," she said to Olbeck.

"Let's walk around, there must be another way."

"We could break it down."

Olbeck hesitated. "Let's–" The door began to open, slowly and creakily.

The Brigadier stood on the threshold, blinking at them. "Yes?" he said, screwing up his eyes against the brightness of the day after the dimness of the hallway.

Kate held up her warrant card.

"Police, sir. We urgently need to speak to your daughter."

"Yes?"

He hadn't moved. Kate made a noise of impatience and pushed past him into the house. She looked up at the staircase and there, frozen on the top step, was Rebecca D'Arcy-Warner. Their eyes locked.

"Rebecca–" Kate began and then the woman on the stairs whirled around and ran.

Kate didn't stop to think. She let her legs carry her up the staircase, her arms pumping, heart racing. She heard Olbeck shout something, but by that time she was up on the landing. A door slammed at the far end of the corridor.

Kate ran quickly down the hall and wrenched open the door. Inside was a bedroom, with the unlived stillness of a guest room. Rebecca appeared to have disappeared into thin air. Kate bent down and checked under the bed. Against the far wall was another door. Bracing herself, Kate yanked it open.

Another staircase, a plain wooden one this time. How big was this house? Kate's heart was thumping. She knew she should wait for Olbeck, the two of them should go together, but she couldn't. She ran up the stairs, past a large window. Outside, she could see Theo's car drawing to a halt, scattering gravel. She ran on, through another door and into another corridor. She seemed to be in the upper stories of the house now. She stopped for a second, holding her breath and trying to listen above the rushing of blood in her ears. Above her head, a floorboard creaked.

She opened a door to an empty room, save for a drift of cardboard boxes in the corner. She tried another door which led to a small and shabby bathroom. This was hopeless. Rebecca could be anywhere. Her radio crackled, making her jump.

"Where the hell are you?" Olbeck hissed at her over the airwaves.

"Don't know. Have you spotted her?"

"The Major says there's an attic, a big one. We're coming up. Wait for–"

"I don't have time to wait!"

"Kate–"

She'd turned and started running again.

She found another corridor after the third door she tried opened. This was a smaller hallway, uncarpeted and ending in a small, steep flight of steps. Kate pattered along. The stairs ended in yet another door. Kate went through it and stopped dead.

She was standing in a small, white-painted room with a cream carpet. There was a cot. There was a Moses basket. There was a white-painted chest of drawers, with baby clothes stacked along the top. There was Rebecca D'Arcy-Warner standing at the far end of the room, a sleeping baby in her arms.

Kate stood stock still. She breathed out slowly.

"Charlie," she said.

Rebecca's eyes were fixed on her face. She was standing by another door, a small one, barely half the size of a normal door. Keeping her eyes on Kate, Rebecca extended a free hand and turned the handle of the door.

"Rebecca," said Kate. "I can help you. Please give Charlie to me."

Rebecca said nothing. Her face was a curious, blank mask, devoid of expression. She stooped, never taking her eyes off Kate and bent to get through the small doorway.

"Wait–" said Kate, moving forward, but Rebecca and the baby were gone.

Kate rushed forward and crouched, pushing herself through the doorway. She straightened up and realised she was on the roof of the house. This part was flat, covered with some sort of tarred covering. The wind hit her, whipping her ponytail up. She looked around wildly. Rebecca and Charlie were standing by the edge of the roof, where a tiny iron balustrade provided no stability at all against the long drop. Rebecca's red hair swirled around her face, and Charlie's blanket fluttered in the wind.

Kate inched forward. Rebecca took a step nearer the edge of the roof.

"Wait," said Kate. Her voice was shaking. "Just wait. I can help you."

Rebecca said nothing.

"Look," said Kate. "I'm stopping right here. I won't come any closer. Why don't you come over here a bit and we can talk? We can talk about anything you want to talk about."

Rebecca remained silent.

"We can talk about Charlie, if you like. Or Nick. Or anything. Why not just come over here a bit and I can help you with whatever it is you need help with."

"Nick," said Rebecca suddenly. Her arms tightened about Charlie. "*Nick.*"

"You must be very angry with him."

Rebecca made a gasping noise, air rushing inwards.

"Angry? Angry doesn't even come close to it. Do you know what it feels like to lose the chance of having a child? To wait and wait for your partner to grow up and want to be a father?"

"That must have been so hard," said Kate. She took a tiny step forward and then another.

"*Ten years* I waited for him to propose. Ten years, I waited for him to give me a child. Ten years of watching my fertility just drain away. He kept fobbing me off. He kept telling me 'one day.'"

"That's so cruel," said Kate, stepping a little bit nearer.

"I just waited and waited. Don't rush him, I told myself. Don't rush him. All the while, it was just getting harder and harder. We used to go to weddings... other people would get married, but not us. I used to have to watch other women get married, have babies, everyone was having babies – but not me. I kept thinking there was still time. Do you know what it's like to watch your chances just evaporate into thin air? Whilst everyone else around you gets what they want?

"I know," said Kate, holding out her hands, palm up. "I know."

"He was such a *child*. That's what he wanted – a mother. That's why he was with me. He knew I'd mother him. He just kept fobbing me off!"

"I'm sorry, Rebecca."

"He robbed me!"

"It must have been so awful for you," soothed Kate. She looked at Charlie, sleeping so peacefully in his kidnapper's arms. One little hand opened and closed like a starfish.

Rebecca suddenly seemed to become aware that Kate had nearly reached her. She gasped and stepped nearer the edge.

"Wait!" said Kate. Her stomach churned. "I can help you. I know you don't want to hurt Charlie, do you?"

Rebecca looked down at the baby. Her face contracted for a moment.

"I never meant any harm," she whispered.

"You're fine, you're fine," said Kate, shivering in

the cold wind. "I can help you. Won't you give me Charlie to hold for a moment?"

Rebecca tightened her grip.

"Ten years," she said. "Ten years of being told he wasn't interested in marriage and children. And within a year he'd married someone else and was a father."

"It's so hard," said Kate. She held out her arms. "Why not let me hold Charlie for a bit? Or shall we take him back inside? It's getting cold out here. Don't you think we should take him back inside?"

Rebecca was trembling

"I knew the security code," she said. "I knew the number he used. You'd think most people would use something like their birthday or their *loved one's* birthday. That would be the normal thing to do." She laughed a mirthless laugh. "Nick used the date he made his first million." She laughed again and the laughter trailed off into something that was closer to a sob.

"You poor thing," said Kate. "Let's go inside, shall we? Shall I hold Charlie for a bit?"

Rebecca didn't seem to have heard her. She was staring down at Charlie's peaceful face.

"I only wanted what was mine," she said. "He's mine. He should have been mine."

"Of course he is," said Kate. "He's beautiful. Could I hold him for a second?"

She held her breath. Rebecca stared at the baby.

Then she slowly extended her arms. Kate inched forward, barely breathing. She felt the light weight of the baby and slowly, oh so slowly, drew him towards her.

"He's a beautiful baby, Rebecca," she said, her voice shaking. She didn't dare step backwards yet for fear that Rebecca would grab him back. "He's so lovely."

Rebecca looked at the baby wrapped in his blankets. She put one finger out – Kate managed not to flinch – and touched the baby's firm little cheek. He turned his face towards the touch, making little sucking motions with his tiny mouth.

"Charlie," whispered Rebecca.

Then she turned and stepped off the edge of the roof, lifting her feet to clear the iron balustrade. Kate heard her intake of breath as she stepped out into nothingness, into the void, but there was no sound, no scream as she fell, no sound at all until her body hit the ground far below.

Chapter Twenty One

ANDERTON LOOMED ABOVE THE TABLE, carrying a tray filled with clinking glasses.

"Your cranberry juice, DS Redman " he said, placing the drink in front of Kate. "Don't drink it all at once."

"I won't."

"Sure you don't want a proper drink, DS Redman?"

"For Christ's sake," snapped Kate. "Just call me Kate, all right?" Anderton said nothing. "Sir," she added.

He grinned and gave her a strange look, wry and approving at the same time, as if she'd passed some sort of secret test.

"Cheers," said Olbeck, clinking his pint glass against Anderton's and then against Kate's dainty pink drink.

They all drank for a moment and, in unison, put their slightly emptier glasses back on the table.

There was a moment's silence, broken only by

the beeping of the slot machine in the corner of the pub.

"How did she think she was going to get away with it?" said Kate, knowing someone would have to start, and it may as well be her.

"Public school arrogance," said Olbeck. "They think they're invincible. They are never wrong."

Kate raised her eyebrows at him.

"I know," he said. "I went to public school."

Kate was intrigued, but this wasn't the time to pursue it. She turned to Anderton.

He turned his pint glass around slowly, inking wet rings of condensation into the scarred table top.

"The backdrop, shall we say, to this case goes back a long way," he said. "Back ten years ago, at least, when Rebecca D'Arcy-Warner was rich, some would say beautiful, successful and in love with Nick Fullman. She had everything she wanted except the one thing she really wanted, the thing she thought would come naturally. The one thing that she naturally assumed would be the next thing on the list."

"A baby," said Anderton. "But no baby was forthcoming. She pressed Fullman about it, about marriage too, although I'm willing to bet that she would have had the baby with him without the marriage certificate, if it had come to that. But the fact was, Nick Fullman didn't want a wife and he certainly didn't want a baby. We can speculate why he and Rebecca got together in the first place, but after ten years it was clear that Nick Fullman had no intention of changing the status quo. Perhaps he wanted a mother figure, having lost his own mother so young. Who knows? What he didn't want to be was a father."

Kate raised a finger. "She said that – Rebecca – something about him needing a lot of mothering. She told me that."

Anderton looked at her and nodded slightly, before continuing.

"Rebecca and Nick eventually got engaged. Was this after a lot of pressure from Rebecca? A lot of emotional blackmail? Who can say? I'm sure to Rebecca this meant that she could finally see the end prize in sight – marriage and a baby. But as we all know, from Nick's stepmother Evie, he had no intention of actually going through with the marriage. It was a sop to Rebecca's feelings – some might say a calculated move to keep his life on the calm, even keel he wanted it to be–"

"Didn't want to lose his rich girlfriend, more like," said Olbeck.

"Maybe. Maybe. Whatever the reason, Nick Fullman had no intention of marrying Rebecca and no intention of having a child with her, in or out of wedlock."

"Bit of a bastard, wasn't he?" said Olbeck.

Anderton looked at him.

"Was he? Perhaps. He's not the only man to not want to rock the boat, to be happy with his life as it is. Perhaps he was fooling himself as well as Rebecca. Perhaps he thought he'd change his mind."

"Perhaps he didn't want to hurt her," said Kate.

Anderton nodded.

"The road to hell, and all that," he said. "Hey, Mark? Sound familiar?"

Kate was astonished to see Olbeck blush and drop his eyes to the table. There was an awkward moment of silence before Anderton began speaking again.

"Like so many people stuck in a mediocre relationship, Nick Fullman didn't do anything drastic until he'd actually met someone else. He met Casey Bright at a media party and they fell in love, or lust, or whatever you want to call it. And of course, that gave him the impetus to finish, finally, his relationship with Rebecca."

"Typical man," said Kate. "Won't jump ship without a life raft waiting for him. They never just *leave*. It's always for someone else."

Anderton tipped back the last of his pint.

"You may be right there, DS – Kate. Whatever reason Nick had, it came as a total shock to Rebecca. She was devastated. I think it wouldn't be too far off to say that she almost lost her mind over it. In one fell swoop, she'd lost her partner, her upcoming marriage and of course, any chance of a baby as well."

Kate cleared her throat.

"She could have – couldn't she have tried something else?"

"She tried adoption."

Kate felt her face grow hot, not so much because she was embarrassed – she was over that now – but because she knew the men would *think* she was embarrassed. She drank the remainder of her drink to hide her confusion.

"She tried to adopt," repeated Anderton. "But as we know, she was turned down. We've had a look at her medical records. She had a history of depression, a suicide attempt at university – what they call a passive attempt, a cry for help, but still – and digging deeper, there were other indications of mental instability. She had a history of self-harming. Nick Fullman confirmed that."

"And then, of course, Nick and Casey had a baby. That must have been the straw that broke the camel's back. This man, who'd avoided marrying her for so many years, had robbed her of her chance for a family, goes and marries someone he'd known for a matter of months – weeks, even. And they have a baby. To Rebecca, that must have been the tipping point."

Kate got up and bought the next round of drinks.

Anderton waited until she'd sat down again before he continued speaking.

"She planned it carefully. She knew the security codes to the Fullmans' house and she probably knew where the CCTV cameras were as well. She had money, a lot of money, and we all know how much you can do – can get away with – if you have money. And perhaps she had something even more valuable – someone on the inside who would help her."

"Gemma," said Olbeck.

Anderton nodded. "Gemma was obsessed with her boss, Nick Fullman. They had slept together, of course, early on in their working relationship. Poor Gemma was in love, or lust, with Nick and hated Casey. Perhaps she thought that with Charlie out of the way, the Fullmans' marriage would break up, and she'd be left to pick up the pieces. Who knows? Perhaps she just wanted the money."

"It was Rebecca who paid her, then?"

"Yes. Whether Rebecca cooked up this plan together with Gemma or whether Gemma just twigged that it must have been Rebecca, is something we'll possibly never know. I'm inclined to believe that Rebecca *didn't* include Gemma in the plan from the start, but once Charlie had gone, Gemma started to do a bit of digging. She had access to a lot of information through Nick Fullman's business interests. Perhaps she went to see Rebecca and told her that she knew. Who knows? She had Rebecca over a barrel, anyway. Charlie's kidnapping and Dita's death..."

"Yes, Dita," said Kate. "What happened there?"

Anderton gently rolled his pint glass between his hands.

"I think it was accidental. Dita surprised her in the act of lifting Charlie from the cot and Rebecca panicked and hit her with the metal torch she was carrying. She's a tall, strong woman, and she swung as hard as she could. I don't believe she actually set out to kill her. Rebecca was the tall man that Nicholas Draker saw in the woods, of course."

"And the one in the Barbour jacket outside Gemma's flat."

Anderton nodded.

"Rebecca clearly decided that Gemma was too much of a threat. It would have been easy for her to go to Gemma's house on the pretext of paying her next blackmail payment. Then drugging Gemma's drink while she was out of the room and then – well, you know what happened next."

Kate shook her head.

"She must have been mad."

"She thought she had no choice. She can't keep paying off Gemma forever. What was the alternative – losing Charlie, going to prison? She was determined not to lose him. She'd already done so many bad things to get him."

Kate recollected something.

"She said that was what she learned from Nick," she said slowly. "She said something like 'You have to decide what you want and go and get it, no matter what it takes.'"

"Yes. It sounds slightly less admirable if you think about what it really means – stopping at nothing to get what you want, no matter how unreasonable. No matter who you hurt along the way."

"She was obsessed," said Olbeck. "But did she think she was going to get away with it? How was she going to keep hiding him for ever? What about her dad finding him?"

"I think her plan was to pretend that he was hers by adoption. Keep Charlie hidden away in Cudston Magna until the hue and cry dies down and then pretend she's adopted him. She lived a fairly solitary life – there weren't many people to question the arrival of a child in her life anyway. Her father is senile and anything he says can be dismissed as the meanderings of old age. There were no home-helps or carers, of course, coming to the house. Rebecca was the only one there most of the time. Perhaps she planned to get a false passport for him. She knew the Costa brothers. That sort of thing would be exactly the kind of service they'd provide for a fee. She gave us their name in an attempt – another attempt – to make more trouble for Nick Fullman. I don't think I'm exaggerating when I say that the idea of having him found guilty of Charlie's disappearance, possibly under arrest for the murder of his child, was almost as big as incentive as having Charlie himself."

"But there was no body," said Kate.

Anderton shrugged. "I'm not saying he would have been arrested. But Rebecca probably would be happy for him to remain under a cloud of suspicion for the rest of his life."

Olbeck shook his head.

"What a bitch."

Anderton swilled the rest of his pint and stood up.

"Selfishness. That's what every crime comes down to in the end. Selfishness. Someone who thinks what they want is more important than anyone else."

"Yes, sir," said Kate.

Anderton picked his coat. "Good work, though, team. See you tomorrow. Goodnight."

Kate and Olbeck remained silent for a moment after his departure, staring into their drinks, lost in their own private thoughts. Finally Olbeck roused himself.

"Want another?"

Kate shook her head.

"Bedtime for me. I'm knackered."

"I'll walk you back to your car."

The night was cool, a chilly wind blowing. Kate

hunched into her coat, tucking her cold hands under her armpits. They walked in silence back to where Kate's car was parked on a side-street.

"Who was our mystery caller?" said Kate, recalling the missing piece of the puzzle.

Olbeck laughed.

"Disgruntled council worker called Tom Farrow. He'd been made redundant from the planning department and decided to get his own back on the boss. He was the one who sent off the soil samples as well."

Kate nodded. There was a moment's silence.

"Well, goodnight then," said Olbeck.

Kate hefted her keys in her hand.

"What did Anderton mean?" she asked. "When he said something about good intentions to you?"

Olbeck's smile died.

"Oh, you know–"

"No, I don't."

Olbeck shrugged. He had his chin sunk into the neck of his jumper, hunching his shoulders against the cold.

"He's talking about Joe," he said. "He thinks – well – he thinks I'm not being quite fair to him."

Kate's eyes widened. "Him?" she said. Then she laughed. "Oh, sorry. It's not funny. It's just I didn't – sorry."

"Yeah, I'm gay," said Olbeck. "Anyway. Anderton's

right. I'm not being fair. He thinks I'm stringing Joe along a bit. I – well, you know how it is."

"Tell me about it in the morning," said Kate. "Not that my track record with men is anything but disastrous, so don't listen to my advice anyway."

Olbeck grinned. "Night, then."

"Good night."

When Olbeck arrived home, he could hear sounds from the television in the living room. He hesitated outside the door for a moment. He could picture what lay behind the door: a log crumbling to ash in the fireplace, a single table lamp casting a warm golden glow over the room. Joe with his legs thrown over the arm of the chair, a glass of red wine on the coffee table in front of him. A cosy, domestic, harmonious scene. *I don't want that*. The thought was there: immediate, unbidden, inescapable. He sighed and took a deep breath and opened the door.

"You're home early–" began Joe, but Olbeck was already speaking across him.

"Look Joe," he said. "We need to talk."

KATE HAD CIRCLED THE HOSPITAL entrance twice before she spotted her mother, hobbling out towards the entrance, crutch tucked under one armpit. An unlit cigarette held in her free hand. She sighed and drew into one of the parking bays at the front.

"Over here, Mum."

"Thanks, love."

Mary Redman settled herself into the passenger seat and lit up. Kate set her jaw and opened her window.

"How's the ankle?"

"Not too bad. They've given me loads of painkillers. I'll be fine."

Kate thrust away the thought of what those painkillers would be liked mixed with whiskey. *Perhaps I should stay with Mum tonight?* She shuddered inwardly at the thought, and the quick stab of guilt made her say, in softened tones, "I'll see you're fine and settled before I go."

"Thanks, love."

They drove in silence and clouds of smoke for a few miles. Kate was concentrating on finding her way on these unfamiliar streets when her mother spoke up.

"Solved that case, then?"

Kate glanced at her.

"That's right. He's back where he belongs now."

"Thank God," said Mary, comfortably. She rolled down her window and pitched her cigarette butt out. Kate winced.

Back at her mum's place, Kate helped her up the bumpy path and to the sofa, carefully lifting the plastered ankle onto a cushion. She made a cup

of tea, put the ashtray within reaching distance of
Mary and made sure she had a glass of water on the
table. Then she stood back, hesitantly.

"Are you sure you'll be all right?"

"I'll be fine, love. Go on home now. You must be
tired."

Kate still hesitated. "Can you, you know, get to
the loo okay on your own?"

Mary rolled her eyes. "'Course. Look, stop
worrying. Always were such a worrier, weren't you?
Even as a child."

Kate bit back the retort that she'd had to be the
one who worried about things as her own mother
clearly hadn't worried about anything, except where
her next drink and smoke was coming from. She
bit her lip, turning a little. She could see out of
the window into the tiny garden next door, where
washing flapped on a line. Her eyes fastened on one
of the garments fluttering in the wind – a blue and
brown striped babygro.

She kept facing away from her mother, holding
each elbow in her opposite hand.

"Did you – did you really think I made a mistake?"
she said, her voice so faint she could barely hear it
herself. "With – with the baby? Did you really think
I should have kept him?"

There was a silence behind her. Kate kept her
eyes on that tiny piece of clothing, snapping and
flexing in the breeze.

Then Mary said, "You did what you had to, I suppose."

Kate blinked hard. Anderton's words were reverberating around her skull. *Selfishness. That's what every crime comes down to in the end.* Well, she hadn't committed a crime, but she felt as guilty as if she had, She was as selfish as the next person, wasn't she? *Aren't you, Kate?*

"I told myself I was doing it for him," she said slowly, almost to herself. "I told myself it was the best thing for him."

"It might have been."

The babygrow blurred in Kate's vision.

"I did it for me, though," she whispered. "It was what I wanted. I told myself I was doing it for him, but I wasn't."

There was a long moment of silence. Kate took a deep, shuddering breath.

There was the click of the cigarette lighter and the familiar smell of cigarette smoke wending its way up to the tarred ceiling.

"Don't go upsetting yourself," said Mary. "You thought you were doing the best thing at the time. Just like every mum does, love."

When Kate arrived home, she took her usual shower, scrubbing her skin and her hair, washing her sins away. She put on her softest, most comfortable pair of pyjamas. Then, as the kettle boiled, she reached for the box under her bed, the box from her attic. She levered off the box lid, clear from dust now, and reached in. The envelope felt heavy in her hand. Would her boy open it on his eighteenth birthday? She hoped so. She curled herself up on the sofa and put the envelope up to her closed eyes for a moment, steadying herself. Then she opened it, drawing out the many sheets of paper with trembling hands and smoothing them out.

She took a deep breath, and she began to read.

THE END

WANT MORE CELINA GRACE?

REQUIEM
(A Kate Redman Mystery)

WHEN THE BODY OF TROUBLED teenager Elodie Duncan is pulled from the river in Abbeyford, the case is at first assumed to be a straightforward suicide. Detective Sergeant Kate Redman is shocked to discover that she'd met the victim the night before her death, introduced by Kate's younger brother Jay. As the case develops, it becomes clear that Elodie was murdered. A talented young musician, Elodie had been keeping some strange company and was hiding her own dark secrets.

As the list of suspects begin to grow, so do the questions. What is the significance of the painting Elodie modelled for? Who is the man who was seen with her on the night of her death? Is there any connection with another student's death at the exclusive musical college that Elodie attended?

As Kate and her partner Detective Sergeant Mark Olbeck attempt to unravel the mystery, the dark undercurrents of the case threaten those whom Kate holds most dear...

Turn the page to read the first
two chapters of Requiem:

Requiem

A Kate Redman Mystery: Book 2

CELINA GRACE

© Celina Grace 2013

Chapter One

THE GIRL'S BODY LAY ON the riverbank, her arms outflung. Her blonde hair lay in matted clumps, shockingly pale against the muddy bank. Her face was like a porcelain sculpture that had been broken and glued back together: grey cracks were visible under the white sheen of her dead skin. Her lips were so blue they could have been traced in ink. Purple half-moons pooled beneath the dark fan of her eyelashes.

"So, what do you think?" asked Jay Redman.

His half-sister cocked her head to one side. "It's very...powerful," she said cautiously. She reached a finger out toward the scene, realising something.

"It's *not* a photograph, is it? Wow, it looks just like one."

Jay Redman's painting technique was called 'hyperrealism'; it mimicked the precision of a photograph, but the image was delineated in paint. She looked at her little brother with a mixture of affection and exasperation. She appreciated the gesture, and God, Jay had real talent, but what on Earth made him think she'd want a picture of a dead girl hung above the fireplace? It was like looking at a crime scene photograph.

"It's great, isn't it?" said Jay. He adjusted the frame slightly, straightening it like a proud father pulling the shoulders of his son's first school blazer into shape. "Best thing I've done so far."

"Yes, indeed!" said Kate, trying to sound enthusiastic.

"It's for our end of year show. My tutor thinks it's great—he thinks it might even win the Bolton Prize."

"That's the top award, isn't it? That's brilliant, Jay. Why are you giving it to me?"

"I thought you'd like to have it for a while," said Jay, still staring proudly at the painting. "It's a housewarming present. On loan."

"Well, thank you."

"I'm calling it 'Ophelia Redux.'"

Kate felt another burst of affection towards her sibling. How wonderful it was to have someone in the family who knew Shakespeare, who had even *read* Shakespeare. It was clear why she and Jay got along so well, and it was something more than the fact that Kate had practically brought him up. There was no one else in the Redman family and its many offshoots who could talk about things other than reality television and the latest tabloid headlines.

Kate had pulled herself up by her bootstraps, and here was Jay, doing the same, even if the path he was taking was a different one to hers.

"It's great, Jay," she said, and her pride in her younger brother gave her tone a warmth which made her sound sincere. Jay beamed.

"I'm well proud of it," he said, reminding his sister that he did, in fact, have some way to go before he shook off his roots entirely. She gave herself a swift mental kick for being so judgemental.

"It's well good," she said, grinning. "Now, have you seen the rest of the house?"

"Can you show me after a drink?"

"Of course, sorry." Kate headed for the kitchen, still a little unfamiliar with the layout of her new house. She'd been here all of a week, and the rooms were still packed with boxes. "Tea?"

"Haven't you got anything stronger? We *are* supposed to be celebrating your move, you know, sis."

"Um..." Kate opened a few kitchen cupboards hopelessly. There was probably an ancient bottle of wine packed in one of the many cardboard boxes but where, exactly?

Jay rolled his eyes.

"Luckily for me, I know what you're like." He put his hand into his ragged green backpack and pulled out a bottle of champagne with a flourish. "See how good I am?"

"Jay, that's brilliant. How do you afford champagne on a student's budget?"

"Ah," said Jay. "Now there you have me."

"You didn't steal it?" gasped Kate, horrified.

"'*Course* not, sis, what do you take me for?" He leaned forward conspiratorially. "It's not real champagne. Just cheap fizz."

Kate smiled, relieved. "It'll do fine. As long as you don't mind drinking it out of mugs."

"Classy."

"I think you mean 'bohemian.'"

Kate sat on the sofa she'd brought from her old flat, and Jay took the new armchair she'd splashed out on when she moved. They clinked mugs and sipped. Kate found her gaze being drawn to the painting of the girl once more.

"Who's the model?" she asked. She looked at the mock-dead face, noting the fine bones under the unnatural pallor of her skin.

"My mate, Elodie."

There was a casualness in Jay's voice that didn't deceive Kate, especially with all her experience with reading what was unsaid.

"Girlfriend?"

Jay slugged back the rest of his champagne. "Nope, just a mate."

"Right," said Kate. She tipped a little bit more fizz in Jay's mug. "Is she on your course?"

Jay was in his second year at the Abbeyford School

of Art and Drama, a further education college that specialised in the visual and dramatic arts. Kate had been thrilled when he'd decided to study there; her home town of Bournemouth was well over an hour's drive away from her new location, and while Jay had still lived at home, she'd not seen much of him.

"Nope. She's a musician, goes to Rawlwood."

Kate raised her eyebrows. "She must be good, then. They hardly accept anyone there, unless they're the new—um." She groped for a famous classical musician. "A new Stradivarius, or something."

"Eh?"

"I mean, it's really hard to get a place there."

Jay rolled his eyes. "Well, it probably helps that she's the Headmaster's daughter."

"Seriously?"

"Yep. But, actually, she *is* a talented musician, really good. She plays violin in this great band. Lorelei."

"Lorelei?"

"That's the band name. They play sort of folk rock. It's good—" Jay said, seeing Kate's unconvinced look. "Actually, there's a gig on tonight. I meant to tell you. Did you want to go?"

"Tonight?" asked Kate, doubtfully.

"Oh, come on," said Jay. "I know you normally need your plans signed off three weeks in advance before you commit to anything, but come on, sis, it'll do you good. You need to get out sometimes, you know. Start meeting people. Start joining in."

It was Kate's turn to roll her eyes. "I'm not a hermit, you know. I do have a social life."

"I'm not talking about hanging out with all your copper mates. That's not a social life—that's *work*. You need to get out and meet some normal people."

Kate laughed. "You're telling me police officers aren't normal people?"

Jay gave her a wry look and reached for the last of the champagne.

"No, sis, they are not. They are definitely not."

Kate twiddled her mug around in her hands. She'd planned a nice dinner for Jay's first visit to her new house, and then she'd assumed they'd sit in front of the fire and chat. That was what she felt like doing.

But his remark about her needing to know plans weeks in advance had stung a little. Was she really that inflexible? And when was the last time she'd actually *been* out, anyway? Somewhere that wasn't with her friend, and fellow officer, Mark Olbeck? She groped for a memory and realised that it must have been sometime in the summer: her friend Hannah's party. And now it was November. *All right, so I've had to organise a move in the meantime but honestly, I'm twenty eight, not eighty eight...*

She put the mug down and made up her mind.

"Sure, let's go. It'll be fun."

"Oh, cool, sis. You'll enjoy it. Elodie's great. You'll like her."

The faraway look in his eyes as he mentioned his friend's name troubled Kate a little. She wondered whether Elodie knew how Jay felt about her. Well, she'd be able to see for herself later.

"Where's this gig?"

Jay tapped his phone's screen and began to scroll through his text messages.

"Arbuthon Green," he announced a moment later. "There's a pub there, the—"

"Black Horse," said Kate, sighing.

"You know it?"

"Yes." There had been several arrests there recently for drug dealing, but she wasn't going to mention that to Jay. So a night out at a dodgy pub listening to a student band? She was glad she hadn't drunk more than a mouthful of champagne; she'd be able to drive now and make a quick getaway if necessary.

"What about dinner?" she asked.

"Plenty of time for that later," said Jay. "I'll shout you some chips if you like."

"Perfect," said Kate ironically, standing up. "Come on." She nearly added 'let's get it over with,' but she didn't want to dampen Jay's obvious excitement. It would be nice to spend some time with her brother, anyway. She hadn't seen him for several months, after all.

"How's Mum?" she asked, once they were in the car and making their way to Arbuthon Green.

Jay looked at her in surprise.

"She's fine. Why? Haven't you seen her lately?"

Kate lifted one shoulder in a non-committal shrug.

"Not very lately. I've been so busy. With the move and everything."

Jay had his knees resting on the dashboard, and he was tapping them with his hands in response to some inner music.

"Mum's all right. She's got some new bloke on the go."

Oh God. Kate recalled some of the other 'blokes.' The fellow alcoholic, the married man, the other married man, the petty thief. She suppressed a sigh.

"What's he like?" she asked as they pulled into the car park of the Black Horse.

"All right, actually," said Jay, sounding surprised. "Seems fairly normal. Not like the others."

"Well, that's odd in itself," muttered Kate, almost under her breath. Then she dismissed her mother from her mind and concentrated on finding a parking space in the busy car park.

The pub was packed, standing room only. Jay and Kate battled their way through to the bar. Kate was already regretting her decision to come. She didn't want to stand up for two hours, shifting her weight from foot to aching foot, drinking warm orange juice and listening to some crappy amateur band. She felt a bit cross with Jay. Months since she'd seen him and now they weren't really going to have a chance to catch up at all...

She bought them both a drink after a long and frustrating wait at the bar. They battled back through the crowds to a spare square foot of space over by the back wall that was rather too near the toilets for Kate's liking.

The noise in the pub made it difficult to talk. There was a moment of silence between brother and sister as they sipped their drinks. Kate looked out at the heaving crowd. Lots of students, couples, noisy groups of young people. Denim, leather, piercings, spiky heels, band T-shirts. She looked down at her neat blue jeans and cashmere jumper in a tasteful shade of beige. Suddenly, she felt acutely out of place. Hot on the heels of that feeling, a much sharper surge of loneliness peaked. She felt totally apart from this raucous, happy crowd; it was as if she were observing them from afar, always on the outside looking in.

That's what being a police officer does for you, she thought, but she knew it wasn't just that.

She caught the eye of a man in the crowd who'd turned to look her way, as if attuned to her sudden emotional state. He looked familiar. She opened her mouth to greet him, looked closer, and shut it again. She didn't know him. Kate sipped her drink, cautiously looking back at the man, who'd turned to face the stage again. He still looked familiar. Kate mentally shrugged. She'd had this feeling before, and it usually meant she'd recognised someone she'd met in the course of her duties. Well, that was one way of putting it. Quite embarrassing, actually, running into someone you'd arrested.

She looked again at the man. He did actually have the faintly disreputable look of someone who might have rubbed up against the police at some point. His bone structure was good, you could even say he was raggedly handsome, but the overall impression was of good looks subjected to the major stressors of time, worry and hard living. He was staring at the stage, sipping a pint. Alone, like her.

No, not like her. She had Jay beside her, after all. She was aware that her brother had suddenly straightened up, quivering a little like a hunting dog spotting its quarry. There was an outbreak of noise from the expectant crowd: shouts, cheers, catcalls. Kate realised the band had made its entrance.

She spotted Elodie at once: blonde hair in an elfin crop which framed her fine-boned face. The girl had a violin in one hand, held casually but expertly against her hip, a bit like an experienced mother holds a baby. There was a male singer, hair a mass of knotty dreadlocks, nose ring glinting under the pub lights. A drummer and a guitarist, again both male, studenty, scruffy.

Elodie tucked the violin under her chin. The singer counted his band members in, and they launched straight into their first number.

Three songs later, Kate was surprised to find that she was actually enjoying herself. The band, despite their scruffy appearance, were polished performers; they were well-rehearsed and talented and still had the charming enthusiasm of an amateur group. The songs were good, alternating between rollicking, stomping pop and quieter, more melodic ballads. Elodie came into her own during the slower pieces, her nimble fingers drawing plaintive, beautiful sounds from the strings of her violin. She played with great intensity, closing her eyes, seemingly lost in her own world of music.

Kate watched her face as she played, noting the high cheekbones and the sharp angle of her jaw. A beautiful girl, and beautiful in an uncommon way. There were plenty of pretty girls in the room, but Elodie had something else, some other quality that drew the eye. No wonder Jay was smitten.

The band finished their set with a rousing, raucous little number that had the crowd cheering and clapping. Elodie flourished her bow, laughing while she took a bow, and then the musicians all left the tiny stage.

Jay turned to Kate, raising his eyebrows. "Pretty good, huh?"

"They were excellent," agreed Kate.

"Let's go backstage, and you can meet her."

They battled their way through to the back of the pub. 'Backstage' was a bit of a misnomer—the band was crammed into a fetid little room just off the corridor, along from the toilets.

Kate was curious to see how Elodie greeted Jay. She was starting to wonder whether Jay actually knew her as well as he had implied, but she had to know him fairly well to agree to something like modelling for his painting, surely?

Her doubts were dispelled as Elodie caught sight of them. She shrieked and hurled herself at Jay, hugging him and landing a misdirected kiss on his ear.

"You came! What did you think? Were we good? Did you see me fuck up that last song? God!"

The questions came rapidly. Kate, ignored for now, could see the manic glitter in Elodie's eyes— the dilated pupils—now that she was close to the girl. Drugs? She really hoped no one would pull anything out in front of her. She'd *have* to arrest them, and then Jay would never forgive her.

Jay was laughing. He turned to her and gestured.

"Sis, this is Elodie. Elodie, this is my big sister, Kate."

"Hello," said Kate, reaching out to shake hands.

"Hi!" said Elodie. She pulled Kate forward into a hug—Kate squeaked in surprise—and kissed her cheek. The girl's body was thrumming with energy, her cheek warm and damp against Kate's.

"I thought you were really good—" began Kate.

"Oh thanks, you know, first nights are always tricky. Totally nerve-wracking."

"You haven't played here before?"

Elodie shook her head, her eyes sparkling. Kate suddenly saw what she must have looked like as a little girl: mischievous and cherubic at the same time, with blonde curls and chubby cheeks.

"Kate's seen the picture of you," said Jay. "You know, *the* picture. She loved it."

Elodie shrieked. "Damn you, Jay, that river bank was cold. And the *mud*...he made me lie in the mud for *hours*."

Even over the hubbub of the crowded room, Kate could hear her beautiful accent, each vowel and syllable falling neatly into place. It was easy to see how Elodie was the daughter of the head of Rawlwood College. Privately educated, loved and cherished, she must have had the best of everything. A girlhood so different to Kate's that it was difficult not to feel a surge of envy.

"So you're Jay's big sister?" asked Elodie. "He often talks about you."

Kate smiled. "All good, I hope." A clichéd response.

"What do you do?"

Kate glanced at Jay, wondering whether

to come clean. Being a police officer—and a detective especially—was like being a call girl or a gynaecologist. People were fascinated, and they wanted all the gory details, but at the same time, they were always a little uneasy in your presence.

"Um—"

She could see Jay shaking his head, a minute gesture easily passed between siblings.

It didn't matter anyway. She could see Elodie had lost interest in her answer; the girl's gaze was drawn up and over her shoulder. Kate watched the light die in Elodie's eyes, noticed the sudden dimming and shrinking of her personality. Elodie's smile faded. She muttered something like 'excuse me a minute' and pushed past Kate and Jay.

Kate turned round. The man she'd noticed earlier was standing in the doorway to the room, and Elodie was walking up to him, talking to him in a voice too low for Kate to make out their conversation. After a moment, they left the room together.

Kate frowned. Sensitive to atmosphere, she could feel the chill settling on the room. There was a sense that the party was over, that the best of the night was gone. She was suddenly aware of how tired she was.

She turned back to Jay.

"Do you want to make a move—" she began, stopping when she saw the bleak look on his face.

"What's wrong?"

Jay seemed to shake himself mentally.

"Nothing," he said, after a moment. She could see him forcing a smile. "I'm alright. Want a drink?"

Kate shook her head. "I'm bushed, Jay, and I've got to work tomorrow. Shall we head home?"

"I'm going to stay on for a bit."

"Really?"

Jay patted her arm. "S'alright, sis. Don't worry about me. You go on home and get some sleep."

"But how will you get back?"

"I'll get a cab. Don't worry."

Kate hunted in her bag before realising she didn't even have a spare key.

"I'll lock up, but just ring me on my mobile when you get back," she said. "I'll keep it by my bed."

"Yeah, cool." From Jay's distracted manner, she wasn't even sure he was listening. He was still staring at the empty doorway where Elodie and her male companion had been standing. Kate wavered for a moment, conscious of a faint nagging feeling of unease. Then she told herself not to worry. Jay was an adult, after all.

"See you later, then. I've made the spare bed up for you."

"Cheers, sis."

He hugged her goodbye, but she could tell his attention was still far away. *Oh well. Bedtime, Kate.*

She looked for Elodie as she walked to her car, thinking she might see her outside the pub door, smoking cigarettes with the little crowd that had gathered there. There was no sign of her. Kate stood for a moment, her hand on the handle of the car door, wondering whether to look for her, to say goodbye and thank you. Then she dismissed the thought.

At that moment, all she wanted to do was get home and climb into her new bed.

Chapter Two

WHEN KATE GOT TO THE office the next day, Olbeck was already there, hunched over his desk staring blearily and uncomprehendingly at the screen. He gave Kate the big, forced smile of a man pretending he didn't have a hangover.

"Good night?" asked Kate.

"Mmmph."

Kate said nothing, but she reached into her desk drawer and drew out a packet of paracetemol, which she threw across the desk.

"I'm *fine*," snapped Olbeck as the packet landed on his keyboard. "Just tired, that's all."

Kate said nothing. Olbeck relented.

"Sorry. Thanks."

Kate got them both a coffee and sat down again. She looked again at the text message from Jay, who hadn't come home last night. *Got a bed sis, wont be hm, c u later xx.* Sent at 4.13am. Whose bed? Elodie's or some random pick-up? Or simply a friend? She tried not to worry. *He's an adult*, she told herself, not for the first time.

She looked across at Olbeck, who was wincing and rubbing his temples. She wasn't going to worry about *him*, either. He was an adult too, although he currently wasn't acting much like one.

Olbeck had split up with his partner, Joe, several months ago. Having been the one to instigate the break-up, Olbeck had been making the most of his newly-found freedom. Night after night, he'd been out clubbing, partying, drinking and dancing. When he wasn't out living it up, he was working all hours, clocking up the overtime, constantly in the office. To Kate, it seemed very much like the actions of a man who was trying not to face up to something painful. However, having had her head bitten off more than once when she'd tried to broach the subject, she'd decided discretion was the better part of valour and was currently keeping her mouth shut.

She dismissed both Jay's and Olbeck's private lives from her mind, mentally squared her shoulders, and turned her attention to the massive amount of paperwork littering her desk while trying to ignore the long-suffering groans Olbeck kept making under his breath.

"What have we got today?"

Olbeck shoved a file across the desk.

"That domestic assault case is coming up."

"I thought Rav was doing that one?"

"He is, but—"

The phone rang. Olbeck picked it up.

"Olbeck here."

He said nothing else, but there was something in the change of his posture that made Kate sit up. She sat with pen poised, feeling her stomach tighten a little. It was a sixth sense, that's what it was; you knew when something big had happened. Olbeck wasn't saying much, just asking a series of blunt questions and scribbling down the answers. He said goodbye and put the phone down.

Kate put her pen down.

"What is it?"

Olbeck stood up, reaching for his car keys.

"Dead girl in the river. Patrol just called it in."

"Oh, no."

"Afraid so. "

"Where?"

"Arbuthon Green."

Kate was reaching for her coat and looked up in surprise. "Seriously? I was there last night. Just last night."

"Should I arrest you?"

"Ha, bloody ha. Come on, you can tell me what you know in the car."

It was a twenty-minute drive to Arbuthon Green, and their route took them past the Black Horse, shut up now at 10.30am in the morning. The pavement outside was littered with cigarette stubs and empty bottles. Olbeck drove on through streets of terraced houses, their walls grey with pockmarked pebbledash and festooned with satellite dishes. Abbeyford was a reasonably affluent town, but every town has its poorer areas. Arbuthon Green was one of them.

The river was a winding oasis of beauty in the squalor. A footpath ran parallel with the water, and the banks were fringed with graceful willow trees, frondy branches dipping into the water. The banks were shallow, covered in patchy grass or thick mud. As Kate and Olbeck walked towards the little knot of people further up the footpath, they could see the pale shape of the body on the bank. No tent had yet been erected to screen the body from public view.

"Where's Scene of Crime?" Olbeck muttered, almost to himself, as they walked along.

Kate said nothing. As they got closer, she was aware of a sensation very much like shock that was beginning to set in. it was worse than shock: a sense of unreality, a feeling of dislocation. She could see the girl properly now; she was lying on her back, arms outflung. There was mud in her blonde hair, and her face was blue-lipped, ghastly pale.

"Oh my God."

Olbeck turned as Kate stopped walking.

"What's wrong?"

Kate was staring at the body. For a moment,

she wondered whether she was still at home in bed dreaming.

"The body...it's the scene—"

"Kate, talk to me. You're not making sense."

Kate turned a pale face to Olbeck. "I know her. The girl. I met her last night."

Olbeck's face mirrored the shock on her own.

"You're kidding."

They'd reached the scene now. There were several uniformed officers, a shivering man in a wet tracksuit and Theo Marsh, one of Kate and Olbeck's colleagues.

Behind Theo, Olbeck saw the white vans of the Scene of Crime Officers draw up.

Theo raised a hand in greeting, and then frowned when he saw Kate's expression.

"What's up?"

Kate was breathing deeply, trying to get a hold of herself. She kept seeing the painting hanging even now on her living room wall: Elodie's mock-dead face, her blue lips. All brought to reality right in front of her. How was it possible? She brought a hand up to her face, pinching the bridge of her nose hard.

"First time, is it?" one of the uniforms asked in a bored and patronising manner.

"No, it bloody isn't," snapped Kate. She wheeled on one heel, not waiting to hear his response, and walked rapidly away along the riverbank. She took just ten steps before stopping, but it was enough to take her away from the body. The feeling of unreality receded slightly. She stood, back turned to the scene, watching the ripples on the surface of the river. Sticks and rubbish had drifted up against the muddy banks. Half a pumpkin floated by, one carved eye socket and several grinning teeth still evident, reminding Kate that Halloween had come and gone.

She heard Olbeck and Theo walk up behind her.

"Kate? You all right?"

She turned round. SOCO had already begun to cordon off the riverbank. The man in the wet tracksuit was being shepherded towards a waiting police car.

"I'm all right. It was just a shock."

"Mark says you know her," said Theo. He looked worried and young. This was a situation they'd discussed before, over drinks. *What if the victim was someone you knew? What would you do?*

Kate opened her mouth to tell them about the painting—and then shut it again.

"I met her last night for the first time. She's called Elodie. She's a musician, goes to Rawlwood College." She remembered what Jay had told her. "I think her father's the headmaster there."

Olbeck's eyebrows went up.

"God. If you're right, this is going to be..." He didn't need to elaborate to his colleagues.

"Are you sure it's her?" asked Theo. "I mean, if you've only met her once and with the water damage, and all..."

Kate was conscious of a sudden spurt of hope. How wonderful it would be if it *wasn't* Elodie. *Wonderful? Listen to yourself, Kate. You're talking about someone's daughter, someone's child.*

She dismissed her inner critic and walked up to the tape line, staring at the body. Once again, she was reminded of the painting. The posture, her face. Was it possible that the painting had actually caused her to misidentify the body because of the resemblance? Kate looked closer and her heart sank. It was definitely Elodie.

She walked back to the others, shaking her head.

"As far as I can see, it's her."

"Shit," said Theo. "We'd better tell Anderton as soon as he gets here."

"He's on his way now?" asked Olbeck.

Theo nodded. Kate watched the river slipping slowly past. She hadn't thought this far ahead yet. Anderton was the DCI for Abbeyford and surrounding areas; he was Kate's immediate boss. He would have to know about the picture. He would have to know everything. Kate remembered Jay sitting across from her on her new chair, tipping his mug full of champagne towards her, smiling.

Who's the model? My mate Elodie.

"Kate?"

Kate realised she was standing with her eyes tightly shut. She gave herself a mental shake. *Get it together. You have no idea what's happened as yet, so stop panicking.*

"Here's Anderton," she said as she saw his car draw up, pleased her voice sounded so normal.

The three of them walked towards their DCI. Anderton had just returned from holiday—three weeks at his holiday home in the South of France, Olbeck had explained to Kate—and he was certainly tanned, his grey hair lightened by the sun. But he didn't look much like a man who'd enjoyed three weeks of relaxation. His brows were drawn down in a frown and there were dark circles under his eyes. *Probably doesn't want to be back at work, and who could blame him?* thought Kate as she returned his subdued greeting.

"Suicide, murder or accident?" said Anderton as they walked back towards the crime scene.

"We don't yet know, sir," said Kate. She pictured the painting hanging on her living room wall and heard her voice falter a little. When was she going to have to mention it?

"Well, any ideas at all? What have you people been doing all morning? Have I just been dragged down here to stand around like a spare part?"

Kate flinched under his tone. He could be brusque, she knew that, but he was not normally so rude.

"A jogger discovered the body at about eight thirty this morning," said Olbeck, hastily. "He thought someone was drowning, waded in and pulled them out, although obviously the girl was long dead by then."

"So the body was found in the river?"

"That's right, sir."

Kate grabbed Olbeck's arm. "Is that right? The body was pulled out of the river?"

"Yes," said Olbeck, looking down at her hand on his arm with a quizzical expression. "Didn't I say?"

"No, you bloody didn't!"

All three men were now looking at her strangely. Kate tried to pin a neutral expression on her face and tried not to show the waves of warm relief washing over her. The resemblance of the body on the riverbank to the picture on her wall was coincidental, that's all. Oh, wonderful relief. For a moment, she felt dizzy with it.

"Something wrong, Kate?" Anderton spoke in a voice that implied she had to tell him.

Kate struggled and managed to subdue her euphoria. "Sorry sir, nothing wrong. I just hadn't been informed of all the facts, that's all." Olbeck shot her a hurt look, which she ignored. "I wasn't aware that this wasn't the original crime scene."

Anderton exhaled in disgust.

"You lot are not impressing me this morning. Theo, tell me something useful, for Christ's sake."

"Yes, sir." Theo almost stood to attention. "As Mark said, the body was discovered by a jogger, Mark Deedham, this morning at about eight thirty. He often runs along this path, according to him. He said he saw something in the water—in fact, he said he saw 'someone' in the water—and thought they were drowning, plunged in, dragged them out onto the river bank and then realised they were, well, dead already."

"Humph." Anderton looked over at the police car where the man in the wet tracksuit had been taken. "That's *his* story. We'll have to take a much more detailed statement. Anything else? Do we know who the victim is yet?"

Olbeck nudged Kate's arm and she shot him an annoyed look. Anderton intercepted it. "Kate Redman, what is the matter with you this morning? Do you know who the victim is, or not?"

Kate spoke. "Yes sir. She's a young student called Elodie, I'm not sure of her last name." Olbeck nudged her again. "For fuck's sake, Mark! Let me finish. She's a musician, a student at Rawlwood College."

Anderton studied her face.

"And how do you know all of this?"

Jay's face swam in front of her eyes. Kate swallowed. "Because I met her last night, sir."

Anderton's grey eyes regarded her steadily.

"Is that so?" he said. "Well, you'd better tell me all about it."

Buy **Requiem**
(A Kate Redman Mystery: Book 2)
on Amazon Kindle, available now.

Acknowledgements

MANY THANKS TO ALL THE following splendid souls:

Chris Howard for the brilliant cover designs; Brenda Errichiello for proof-reading and editing; Lynda Kelly for extra proof-reading; beta readers and lifelong friends David Hall, Ben Robinson and Alberto Lopez; Ross McConnell for advice on police procedural and for also being a great brother; Kathleen and Pat McConnell, Anthony Alcock, Naomi White, Mo Argyle, Lee Benjamin, Bonnie Wede, Sherry and Amali Stoute, Cheryl Lucas, Georgia Lucas-Going, Steven Lucas, Loletha Stoute and Harry Lucas, Helen Parfect, Helen Watson, Emily Way, Sandy Hall, Kristýna Vosecká; and of course my gorgeous Chris, Mabel, Jethro and Isaiah.

This book is for my Mum and
Dad, with love and thanks.